The Kristovas

Judel B. Nuique

Ukiyoto Publishing

All global publishing rights are held by

Ukiyoto Publishing

Published in 2025

Content Copyright © Judel B. Nuique

ISBN 9789370092617

All rights reserved.

No part of this publication may be reproduced, transmitted, or stored in a retrieval system, in any form by any means, electronic, mechanical, photocopying, recording or otherwise, without the prior permission of the publisher.

The moral rights of the author have been asserted.

This is a work of fiction. Names, characters, businesses, places, events, locales, and incidents are either the products of the author's imagination or used in a fictitious manner. Any resemblance to actual persons, living or dead, or actual events is purely coincidental.

This book is sold subject to the condition that it shall not by way of trade or otherwise, be lent, resold, hired out or otherwise circulated, without the publisher's prior consent, in any form of binding or cover other than that in which it is published.

www.ukiyoto.com

Dedication

This book is for every dauntless heart out there that is willing to defy tradition and society. Above all, this is for Ma. Ysabela Louise M. Martinez and Sarrah Jane C. Magdaraog whose existence made a great impact on me.

Contents

Chapter One	1
Chapter Two	7
Chapter Three	19
Chapter Four	27
Chapter Five	35
Chapter Six	44
Chapter Seven	58
Chapter Eight	68
Chapter Nine	80
Chapter Ten	92
Chapter Eleven	101
Chapter Twelve	112
Chapter Thirteen	120
Chapter Fourteen	130
Chapter Fifteen	137
Chapter Sixteen	143
Chapter Seventeen	155
Chapter Eighteen	163
Chapter Nineteen	170
Chapter Twenty	175
Chapter Twenty-One	181
Chapter Twenty-Two	187
Chapter Twenty-Three	193

| Chapter Twenty-Four | 199 |
| Chapter Twenty-Five | 205 |

| *About the Author* | *215* |

Chapter One

Kristova Mansion received a permanent guest one evening. It had been two decades since the house closed its doors to everything, and everyone, because of a scandal which shook two houses many years ago. Yet a family would always be family and the guests were very close relatives.

Juliet Kristova brought her children with her as she fled from a war zone. Rudolf Kristov, her husband, instructed her to do so before the country lost the war and they could suffer horrible things from the enemy, such as beheading or slavery. Being an obedient wife, Juliet just did what Rudolf commanded and found refuge at the doors of Madam Kristova, his only aunt in the capital. Though Juliet bore the face of a desolate woman, she still had the beauty one could merely dream of having.

The possessor of Kristova Mansion, who was called Madam Kristova, welcomed Rudolf's family with open arms though she was downhearted to take the awful news about the war and why he had the need to be left there. Yet she never failed to calm the woman her nephew loved. By then, as she watched her nephew's wife and her grandchildren, she accepted her fate to be the one responsible for their welfare, beginning that night, if the worst-case scenario would, God forbid, occur.

Madam Maria Kristova just reached five-and-forty at the time Rudolf's family arrived. She was the youngest and the only girl among the seven Kristov children. She left her birthplace in exchange for a life she could own and was living very well despite her misadventures in the past. She built a huge house, had widespread connections, hatred from a few families, and almost everything, except for one, a family of her own. However, the arrival of her nephew's family brought her just that, and the sight of her granddaughters for the first time, after knowing them only in letters, made her the happiest woman that instant.

Katarin and Antonia were in their twenties when they appeared before Madam Kristova. Though they were still babies to Maria's eyes, she believed they would be the talk in the capital. They had the beauty which would captivate many eyes, particularly the eyes of gentlemen. The two young ladies had the same physique, for they were twins. They had the face, the curls and even the freckles which would lead you to never distinguish one from the other. But of course, there would be differences, even a bit. And that was being a raven-haired of the former, then the redhead of the latter. Yet Maria reckoned there was more to what she was seeing. After all, it was their first meeting.

Within a week, news circulated around the capital about what happened at Kristova Mansion, for it was a place of talebearers and gossip-mongers. Each individual was required to be ahead concerning the latest rumors and scandals which were happening every day in the busiest region of Simetra. Everyone was then torn to be aware of the struggles at the garrisons of their country. It had been a year since outlanders had been trying to own a part of Southern Simetra, which was rich in gold and wine. And it would only be a matter of time before their men in the capital were ought to be required to fight for the war as well.

"But that's not the only thing which set foot at the mansion a week ago," a gentleman whispered to his companion in a barroom.

"Stop it, Richard. I do not wish to know more about that house. The war is enough to scare me to the bone," warned another who was a good-looking gentleman himself while being cautious of his surroundings. His eyes meandered here and there.

"You should be scared that unmarried ladies are unavailable in the market these days." Richard was eager to lure his companion to something he was surely worthy to be seen like gems of different kinds in a treasure chest.

"Parting because of death is much terrible for me to imagine, my friend," was the remark of the companion. "And please, do not treat women as if they are commodities to be bought anytime, or anywhere. They are humans, too. Rational and clever, just like us."

"Weak but sly, I say," he smirked yet he beseeched, "Hear me out for a second, Elric, please!"

Elric nodded subtly in return with his eyes keenly observing the other individuals in the barroom. Some men and women were publicly displaying their affection, something he loathed seeing. Some looked like they were withering and fading away, as if life did worse to them. He never liked barrooms, particularly that one, but it was the safest place where his uncle would not find him. He had been trying to portray as the good son in the house which built him.

"That mansion sent a letter for the Queen's Ball," Richard whispered again as if the information was confidential enough to be heard by unwanted ears.

Elric said nothing after hearing such and hid his curiosity under his shoes, because the topic had been forbidden for him to talk about nor be curious of.

Richard's brows rose. "Are you not even baffled?"

"No," Elric answered without hesitation. "Not at all."

"That is unbelievable, Elric!" Richard exclaimed. "You see, that house had been hiding from the public. But now it is starting to open its doors for everyone to see. That itself is an invitation. They even say the madam of the house is a beauty herself. I expect the same for the rest of the women inside the mansion."

"Women? Do you mean the maidservants as well? I hate your corrupted mind, my friend. I truly do." Elric laughed quietly before he added, "So, please, let us not indulge ourselves more about this topic. I feel like I am committing a crime."

Another man greeted them as he joined their table before Richard could say more to Elric's words. "Who will accompany me tomorrow evening?" he then asked, still referring to Kristova Mansion Elric tried to forget about.

"I will! It would be my pleasure, Wilfred." Richard was very transparent in his eagerness while Elric only showed indifference.

Wilfred smiled. "That's what I thought."

The three men had been a group since they met, and they were inseparable. When they were together women never failed to give them the attention they had not needed, which they amused themselves of. Elric was an exemption though, for he was the aloof one and seemed to be unapproachable. He actually frowned at the thought of marriages only for mutual benefits, survival to be exact, and no love in it. He better be left alone than marry a woman who would only desire him because of his house.

"And Elric?" Wilfred inquired even though he was quite certain what his dear comrade's answer would be.

"His uncle will kill him if he will know," amused Richard.

"Do not let him know then. Besides, we will just take a glimpse of everything," Wilfred insisted.

Richard laughed. "A glimpse. Of everything. Are you certain?"

"Wilfred, what is this all about really?" Elric was curious as to why his favorite fellows were so motivated at the sudden opening of doors at Kristova Mansion.

"You will know," he gave a teasing smile, "when you will come."

Chapter Two

Katarin was in her room when she overheard the maidservants talking outside her door about a visit at the mansion that night. She agreed with her senses that the two were giggling throughout the conversation.

"Oh, I've heard Mr West is a very handsome man!"

"He is! I wonder if his comrades will accompany him. His group is truly a stunning sight to behold."

"Is that so?"

"Certainly! And I have heard they are seeking wives this year."

"Is that good news?"

"Sadly not, but it is good gossip. Who do you think will be the poor women willing enough to love them? Or, perhaps, save them?" The maidservant was grinning as she said, "One is vain," imagining Richard. "Another is proud," she added, thinking of Wilfred. "And then there is the other who is always both," she laughed, seeing Elric clearly in her memory.

Before Katarin's mind ended up puzzled very much, the voices faded and in a sudden there was a knock on her door. Her mother stood before her as she opened it, requesting her to change into a proper attire for her uncle's presence. She did not ask about the uncle she had never known and followed her mother's instructions hastily. She instead believed for things to be somehow unpredictable in the capital at all times. And that she must always expect the worst.

The next time her mother sprung was because Antonia was nowhere to be found. Katarin smiled at the thought before answering, "Maybe she's in the library." For sure her twin sister was out there somewhere again, and the mansion's library was one of those places. It was a good thing if she was in the library though. But if not, she would be reprimanded for the millionth time as soon as she'd be back from an adventure. Adventure it was as she always preferred calling her escapades that way.

Katarin was the more normal twin as their mother would say, since she was the wife material. She loved cooking, sewing, being alert for occasions, and organizing household events. Yet her liking on spells and magic, something her mother despised, would discredit her almost perfect qualities to be a homemaker. She even dreamt of having children at an early age. Unfortunately, war happened and her dreams were all flushed into the drain. It would be cruel to want, to dream even, of a family in a time of war. It would be a very tragic sight giving birth to babies only for them to see a world of mess and then suffer in such.

"She will be dead when she is out there again! It has been two weeks and she has been leaving the house without my permission for who knows how many times already. What is she up to exactly?" The mother was worried sick. "If Aunt Maria will know about this, who knows when will we be thrown out of this place? I do not want to cause any trouble in the capital. Not again." Not again, of course, for when she eloped with Rudolf many years ago it made an uproar in the capital and shamed her family. Madam Kristova shared the burden, was blamed for certain, because the man was her nephew. But the love Juliet found was worth the risk and she never regretted her decision because the man she chose loved her and remained to love her ardently.

"Mama," Katarin sighed. "You're not even sure she went out. Last time, she was just sleeping in the gardens." She wanted her mother to calm down, but also to cover Antonia's tracks. Her twin liked drinking at Kristova Mansion's cellar and sleeping all over the place when she's too drunk to find her room. But Katarin decided it would be the last time offering some help to her sister. Antonia was required to grow up.

"But she went to the monastery the first time!" Juliet settled on Katarin's bed.

"To pray, mama, to pray. She is a believer, you see. Don't you like seeing your daughter as a devotee?"

"A devotee who is into wine?"

"It is the study of wine, mama."

"Very laughable!" Juliet did a fake laughter. "I hate her drinking habit. Her sleeping habits as well."

"Oh, mama. She'll soon learn. I promise."

"She is just so Antonia." Juliet closed her eyes out of frustration. "Too wild."

"She is, mama. She is."

Madam Kristova, on the other hand, decided to meet her visitors in her study. The messenger handed a letter later that afternoon about the visitation of Juliet's brother. As expected, the madam could no longer hide a secret from the West lineage in her house. She knew this would happen but had not expected for it to be so soon. It had only been a week since the arrival of the three.

"Madam, the visitors are here," the head maidservant informed.

"Let them in."

The first to enter the room was a young blood from the West Mansion, Juliet's brother. Though his appearance looked lively, there was a little fear in his eyes and Madam Kristova took notice of that. He was later followed by the most unexpected face, a Coldwell. Madam Kristova's countenance turned sour. She wasn't able to hide her disappointment regarding the sight of a Coldwell blood. She hated the master of Coldwell Mansion since time immemorial. However, she admired the dauntless heart of the young lad to step foot inside her house. It had been two decades since a Coldwell ever mingled with a Kristova.

"Good evening, gentlemen!" Madam Kristova greeted.

"Good evening, Madam Kristova," Mr West returned the greeting while his companion just bowed in response and was tongue-tied.

"Take your seats, please, and feel at home." She waved a hand at a tea set with light snacks on the table, offering them something to eat or drink.

Mr West expressed his gratitude towards the host as his companion and he took their seats.

"I believe you are here for your sister, as well as your nieces. They will be here shortly."

"West Mansion is immensely relieved, Madam Kristova, that you took them in."

"It's a responsibility. They are Kristovas after all."

"Well, yes. Of course."

While waiting, Madam Kristova never said a word again. She just kept on drinking tea while glancing at her visitors from time to time. The silence was deafening really. But the madam hated speaking without restraint that even though she wanted to interrogate the two, she controlled herself to never do such a thing. Spilling secrets with your own mouth would always be a terrible thing to do.

As for Mr West, he felt proud of himself to be one of the firsts to see the interior of the mansion after twenty years of denying its guests. Yet if he went there alone, he was sure to feel as if he was a speck of dust trying to soil Kristova Mansion. And his friend, Mr Kovalski, was right. Madam Kristova was a beautiful sight to behold, making the rumors confirmed as more likely to be true, that she was a witch.

The exterior of the house seemed old, but its inside decorations gave a theatrical air, making its madam as its prima donna. Mr Coldwell observed that and was charmed by what the house offered his eyes, but not the madam whom he believed he had seen already in the past. The study, to be specific, was a small museum. The ceiling portrayed the blue sky in autumn, and there was a huge rug in the middle of the room with the map of the world in it. Bookshelves were fixed on the walls while a big globe was standing at a corner. Madam Kristova's study table was on the other side of the room, opposing the couches where they settled. Books in heaps were on the floor and rolled papers were all over the place. The room had two doors.

However, something was able to take Mr Coldwell's attention away from the room's interior design after all, or maybe it was someone since it moved in a while. A dog, perhaps. It was hiding behind the towering books at another corner, closer to the door far from where they were all occupying. He stared at it for long until it moved again. And it had hands, too. Its limbs escaped its blanket which was supposed to be a coat. He wondered if it was a kid, but when he heard Madam Kristova asking him something, he was required to turn to her.

"Pardon me, madam. I wasn't listening." That's when Mr Coldwell was sure he had seen Madam Kristova sometime in the past. And she still looked the same, beautiful but cold.

"You seemed preoccupied, lad. Are you not feeling well?"

"No. I mean, I am well. It's just that, I think—" He looked at the corner again where he had seen something, but it was already gone. But he was sure it moved and it was there a minute ago. Though he believed he was not daydreaming, he had imagined the worst and that was to have started seeing ghosts.

"What?" the madam eyed him sharply. "You think what?"

"I think I must leave now. I have to go. Forgive me for my manners, madam." The lad decided to sweep his existence off from the mansion since he thought it was truly haunted, and the fact that he was feeling guilty to be there added chaos to his conflicting mind. "Farewell," he said.

"Fare well, indeed," Madam Kristova replied before the young man left.

Mr Coldwell took his exit without saying a word to his companion, who became agitated at the scene though remained spellbound by Madam Kristova's beauty. Mr West was staring at her intently which made the madam glare at him, forcing him to look away.

"Forgive me, brother, to have kept you waiting. We were looking for your other niece, but she was nowhere to be found," entered Juliet with Katarin.

Mr West was filled with pride upon seeing the beauty Juliet's daughter possessed. He even wondered for a second if any man would ever be deserving of wanting such a beauty to hold. Yet he was worried if his other niece was in grave danger. "Do we have to report this to the authorities?"

"No. It is not that serious." Madam Kristova eased their worries. "Antonia is still adjusting to this place. I believe she is just around. She is fine, I'm sure." She had seen her youngest grandchild right after the young Coldwell did.

"You are still you, my dear sister." Mr West did not know what to say since it was their first meeting after a very long time, and he was still playing with toys when she left the capital. Yet Juliet remained to have the title as "The Most Attractive Girl in West Mansion Ever Born," making her youngest sibling awestruck as well.

"You are too kind, my dear brother."

"Nonsense. Anyhow, father sent me after Kristova Mansion sent Isabel's office a letter about my nieces joining the Queen's Ball. And also, hearing about your husband's situation alarmed us so. We will continue to pray for his safety and the country's victory."

"Thank you so much, brother. Please tell father I am well. I am sure he is uneasy about the news. And I promise to pay him a visit anytime soon."

"Of course. I will let him know right away."

"Now, Wilfred, this is my Katarin," Juliet introduced her eldest daughter, "the other twin."

"It's good to finally meet you, uncle." Katarin smiled shyly and offered her hand for a shake.

But Mr West hugged his niece instead. "The pleasure is mine, my love. You can call me Wil if you find it awkward to have a young uncle."

"I am used to it. I have a young grandmother too," was Katarin's reply, referring to Madam Kristova, which astonished both Mr West and the madam.

While everyone was gathered in the study to catch up, Antonia dilly-dallied at the front doors. She had been drinking at her great-aunt's cellar again for her wine study. And all she did was sleep everywhere since she started doing so, because she was too drunk and sleepy to go to her room. But drinking wine was one of the things which kindled her lazy bones in the capital, for it was what she was fond of, even in her hometown. The other one which ignited her interest was the monastery where she went to pray for her father's well-being and the country's victory, one time in secret which wasn't a secret anymore.

Antonia never desired to marry, unlike her twin sister, but to travel, write and taste every wine in the world. She was completely the weird one, not the outcast but the one nobody would dare give any of their attention to, as she believed, because of her extraordinary interests, considering she loathed wearing a dress too. The weight's heavy for her while putting on makeup left her feeling like a clown in a circus. She loved horseback riding, fencing, eating a lot and other stuff that only boys were free to do. Though boyish, she had always kept her father's advice. "Do whatever you like as long as it makes you happy and never harms you in return," he would say. She lived for such words and for adventures she was not sure she could do anymore because of the war that's happening at hand.

Antonia's reverie was ceased later by someone who stumbled down the stairs with the face first on the ground. And it was because of her, who was sleeping at the entrance of the house. Yet if the person wasn't running as if escaping a tragedy, everything would have been fine. "Oh, goodness! Are you alright, sir?" she sincerely asked the man, or the boy, yet her hand was slapped after she only tried to feel if the person was still conscious or perhaps alive. She yelped, "What was that for?!"

"Are you a dog?!" he gnarled, which was more of a judgement rather than a query. "You should not be sleeping anywhere!"

"Well, you are blind yourself, sir! Did you see a ghost?" Antonia thought dogs were wonderful creatures but wasn't able to stop herself from commenting harshly as well because the person was hostile in his manner of talking.

The man stood up from the ground with his palm on his right temple, it was bleeding. And it was a horrible sight.

"Oh, good heavens! You are hurt!" gasped Antonia which made the man step away from her as he murmured, "This house is a real mess and rumors are true, witches live here!" But his anger hushed the second he saw her appearance. She seemed shining, as if a bright star in a dark night.

"I'll take that as a praise, sir. But I warn you, you are not welcome here anymore." Antonia frowned at the notion, of being labeled as a witch for causing harm. She began untangling the twigs from her hair, she could not even remember where she got them, and went to the ill-mannered figure after pulling a kerchief from her coat to get rid of the blood from his temple.

"Servants do not get to decide that," the man reminded the girl, or the lady. He knew how to deal with women, but he thought about the one in front of him as a different kind of such figure and was authoritative, too, for a servant. Not to mention she looked like a man because of her clothes and stiff movements. Yet he was certain she was someone he just encountered for the first time, and he hated her that very moment for making him feel indecipherable things. His heart was even leaping out of his chest.

"Your palm is the one that is bleeding." Antonia wrapped his hand using the fabric.

"Were you drinking?" The man asked after an intoxicating scent filled his nostrils, turning his stomach. "Great! You are not even a proper lady to begin with," he added, whispering. However, he engraved on his mind the image of a lady who portrayed a raging fire goddess, making his face look even angrier though he was feeling elated at the demeaning encounter. He hated the red color since he was a child, yet the female figure before him seemed comely enough with her red curls. Thus he felt intoxicated all the more.

"And by saying such accusations makes you think you are a gentleman? You don't even look like one." Antonia left his sight as soon as she mumbled such words on his face and banged the door shut as she entered the house.

The man stood there thunderstruck, where Antonia left him, calming his heart before heading towards the Coldwell Mansion where his uncle was waiting to scold him.

Chapter Three

It was the next day and later that morning when Madam Kristova was informed by her head maidservant that her youngest granddaughter had an ill conversation with the Coldwell guest yesterday. With that, she summoned Antonia to her study.

Antonia was still dressed in her sleeping garments when she met the madam which was the reason why she was given an unsolicited advice to wear a formal attire, because it was never the proper garment for a lady in front of others, even the family.

"So, I heard whispers," the madam began the issue she must be dealing with once and for all. Antonia was guilty already but stayed silent and fixed her eyes on the floor as if she was a child who would soon be punished in the cellar. She adored the idea, though. She called that place as wine dungeon.

"There is this rumor in the house about you and that one guest we had yesterday. Not to mention you did not meet your uncle, Wilfred West."

"I am truly sorry, Aunt Maria, for missing my uncle. And forgive me for sleeping at the main door," Antonia said sincerely.

"About that, please, sleep in your room. That is the place for it, you see."

"Yes, Aunt Maria."

"How's your wine study?"

"You knew?" surprised Antonia.

"It is my house. The ceilings have my eyes and the walls have my ears, darling love."

"As usual, I get drunk every time."

"Who would not be? Wine is made to intoxicate the living. It is not wine if it won't make you dizzy and sleepy," Madam Kristova smirked. "Unfortunately, my library does not contain a lot of books for such interest. Tea is my forte, and a bit of farming."

"I heard the capital library is huge."

The madam nodded. "You should pay a visit to the library soon," she mentioned before looking Antonia in the eyes and asking her, "or have you already?"

"No. I never had the chance. And mother will kill me if I go without her permission. Again."

"Never forget to do that, too."

"I will."

"And that guest," Madam Kristova remembered the topic before she absolutely forgot about it. "You must be warned. Don't ever stay in the same room with a Coldwell, literally and figuratively. People like them will only bring you trouble and their tongues are filled with hatred against our house."

"I pray to never see him again, even his shadow," Antonia uttered, remembering how the gentleman, who wasn't gentle at all, gave her ill feeling and called her a servant.

"Good. Now, Antonia, I will send you to a training school for ladies with your sister anytime soon. You will receive education from a madam I trust regarding the etiquette of a lady."

"But—"

"No buts, my dear," the grandmother smiled. "You, particularly, need the program. Though I am fond of you being yourself, I require the best version of who you are. You will be staying there for two years."

"Two years?" Antonia gasped. "Two years?! That is a long time!"

"For you, yes. However, the Queen's Ball is almost here, which you sisters must attend, so a week before that you'll be trained about balls, dances and social interaction."

"Good heavens, have mercy on me!" But Antonia understood her great-aunt's concerns and everything about the Queen's Ball since it had been the most famous event in the country. Madam Kristova wrote to them about it once. And ladies who joined the ball were expected for betrothal after, but Antonia never dreamt of it. What she wanted was to be just like her young grandmother, a spinster. She had no man in life and she's free. So, for Antonia, she could travel anytime and anywhere if she'd end up just like her.

"I don't need those training sessions to be a proper lady. I don't want to be a lady, nor settle and marry," Antonia confessed. "Aunt Maria, please!"

"But Antonia, I love you so much that I must have you educated about the world. Once you know things and the proper manners about living, you will be able to handle your own life. That is all I can give you while I am alive. You have no other choice, and so do I."

Antonia accepted defeat. "Yes, Aunt Maria."

"I once wanted to register myself at an educational institution, a university," Madam Kristova shared a prior experience, "but women were just not allowed. I hope the future will be more welcoming to their women."

"I pray, too, Aunt Maria. I pray, too."

In the opposite end of the capital Coldwell Mansion stood proud at a hill with the ocean at its back. The master of the house was having his late breakfast because he discovered his nephew's entrance at Kristova Mansion last night. He had eyes everywhere in the capital, especially on his beloved successor. But Elric did not leave his room at an early time to meet his uncle for breakfast which made the old bachelor angry. And when Elric came out of his shell and showed himself to his dear uncle, he had a messy face, leaving anyone to think he had been heartbroken for decades or even for life.

"Bloody thing, Elric!" Master Coldwell hollered. "You better cut those bangs off your face or I will kick you out of this place as soon as I am sick of such a sight!"

"Of course, Uncle Edward," replied Elric, who kept his wounded hand hidden inside his pocket and succeeded. It would be a shame to admit to his uncle that a maidservant did that to him, especially a maidservant of Kristova Mansion.

"One more thing, lad. Didn't I tell you to never associate with the Kristovas?"

"You did. And it is not happening again," Elric confessed. "I witnessed their madness firsthand and I had enough of it. Even their servants are ill-mannered. It is very wise to avoid them as you have said."

Master Edward Coldwell grinned at Elric's words before he saw his nephew leaving the dining hall. He was glad at the lad's realization, to be honest. He thought there was no chance, at all, for the two houses to cross paths again.

That same day a woman who was known as the capital's lady escort was making a commotion at the barroom where everyone was frequently visiting. And as expected, every woman in the room hated her presence and her beauty. But who would not? Every man adored her and was bewitched by her. And rumors had it that her aunt drove her out of her house for the same reason.

"Elisa! I heard you are getting poor now. You're behind on your lodging payments, too." A man with ragged clothes and crooked teeth at an isolated table was smiling at the woman's poor state when she reached the bar. He was one of those who could afford her services but was never given one. That was why he would laugh without remorse if the woman would gain more suffering in life.

"You seem so interested in my awful condition. Are you willing to help this poor but beautiful woman?"

"Nah! My wife will kill me if I do."

"I'll be utterly glad if she will." Her vengeful tongue was her good asset too.

"Why won't you live with your aunt then?" the bartender asked Elisa, giving her a glass of beer for free.

She gave him a wink in return before thanking him. "Unfortunately, I cannot afford to stay at her house. My personality is way too much for her to handle," she added.

"I'd say she hates you and your way of living. It is a very shameful and sinful one," was the unsolicited comment by that ugly man beside Elisa, mocking her all the same. "Terrible, really!"

"And who are you to judge? Even though you're not saying it, I know your mind is currently sinning because of my presence," Elisa smirked as she said so. "So, who's who exactly?"

"Crazy woman!" said the man who was left alone by Elisa, who drank her beer in one go, and the bartender, who paid attention to other customers.

When Elisa exited the barroom, she unexpectedly met Richard Kovalski outside the building. She always admired the man ever since, but he just loved too many women. And she did not have the wealth to lure him to her arms, which was also a great problem of hers at the moment. In addition, she was well aware about the fact that Richard only considered her as a mere acquaintance without the chance of being more to him.

"Miss Pierce!" Richard greeted. "It's nice to see you. How are you?"

"Not good," Elisa honestly replied. "Do you know anyone I can tour around the capital? I badly need the money."

To Richard Kovalski, Elisa's existence brought him pure bliss every single time he took a glance at her. Unfortunately, he never had the courage and the heart to pursue her whenever he wanted. His parents despised Elisa's way of living, and to them, she's a rotten woman. If she was rich, maybe she could have had the chance to seduce his kin, but she was not. And he was too weak to fight for something he could not be responsible for in the end. He was still trying to elevate himself from the gutters.

"I will inform you as soon as someone is in need of your touring." Richard did his very best to hide his admiration for the woman and aced at it.

"Thank you, Mr Kovalski. Until then."

Richard only showed a slight nod before Elisa went her way. He knew he would see her at that exact time during the day in the barroom but never expected for her to leave so soon. It was Elisa's pattern to be there, and he memorized it. The woman always amused people during that day in the place by the stories, funny moments and rumors she collected around the capital. And Richard was one of her fanatics. She was so relieving to see and to listen to, he'd think. Yet Richard only dreamt of asking her to marry him but could not give it reality. If only he was not from an ambitious house he could do whatever he had been wishing for.

Chapter Four

Weeks after the arrival of Madam Kristova's guests, everyone in the capital was surprised by the sudden changes inside her mansion. The house became alive and the lights were lit even at midnight. The madam, too, was seen leaving the mansion frequently. Though the color of her dresses were still in mourning, there was a time she wore pastel colors with accents of flower embroidery.

One afternoon when their party did some walking along Apollo River, some were able to recognize Juliet as a former member of West Mansion. The twin Kristovas were also considered enthralling as they accompanied the two elder beauties.

Men, too, had talks regarding the house. Though war was slowly approaching the capital, the Kristovas eased their worries at some point. Bachelors started to appear along Apollo River just to take a peek at Madam Kristova's party. Some thought she was truly a witch for she seemed to have never gotten old. A few believed she created a beauty product after her addiction on Alchemy. Her twin granddaughters gained attention and were offered great deals on marriages through letters sent in secret to her. But she, being their guardian, frowned on such matters and never gave replies to the letters. She neither wrote a note nor a word. It was not yet time, she believed.

Some women were enraged and envious of the party as well, that even though their dresses looked sorrowful such were still sought in boutiques and dress shops which in turn were all made just for the Kristovas and by Lili Crossman. A few ladies had tried to be friends with the twin sisters, but Maria Kristova's stared daggers put them in their places. The madam could not let everyone in, they must be filtered. Not all had good intentions most times.

Maria Kristova felt anew. She had been staying in her mansion for twenty years and never let the public take a look at her state. This time, she had the need to come out from her shell. Hibernation was now over. It was time to quake the capital and its flawed society. And her only hope was for her family to be accepted by everybody. Though some admired and respected her, she had had enough of all the hatred and condemnation from others.

Juliet Kristova was joyous to be in the capital again. She had been away for more than two decades when she married Rudolf and had children. She was not able to visit, because she was pretty occupied with farm matters and was busy taking care of her twins. She was also not on good terms with her family at the time yet. She witnessed the capital again with her bare eyes, and she wished to be visiting the place with her daughters even when the countryside would recall them.

Katarin Kristova was highly pleased. It was her first time in the capital and there were multiple things to observe. The dresses were exquisite, porcelain wares were everywhere, and a variety of fabrics existed. Her hometown was all farm and animals and nature. Everything in the capital was new and good to her senses. She prayed to live there if it was possible. She thought it was her rightful place.

Antonia Kristova was the odd one, however. For she was dreadful from the walks, tea parties, heavy dresses and huge hats. Though the capital seemed magical, her hometown was where her heart belonged. She missed walking barefoot, playing on the stream, wearing pants and cardigans, running to and fro, and drinking wine her father made. That was why she never failed pleading to every angel above in the heavens to stop the war, because she utterly wanted to go back home.

"We won't be walking along the river today," Madam Kristova informed her party another afternoon while they were having tea.

"Have you changed your mind about the walk? Are we not going anymore, Aunt Maria?" asked Juliet.

"Oh, no. That's not it. We will be at Lili Crossman's home. She wanted us to grace her gardens."

"Isn't she the famous designer, Aunt Maria?" inquired Katarin with enthusiasm.

"Yes, darling, she is. And she will let us see her tulip collection, too."

"I hope she will be offering us wine instead," Antonia mumbled without noticing her great-aunt hearing her.

"She will," whispered the madam.

"Can I wear pants, too?"

The madam smiled. "If you insist."

Lili Crossman marveled when she saw the Kristovas outside her house. "Mary, finally! We can talk in person and not on paper anymore."

"I think it is the right time, Lili. I have my nephew's family with me. And you will be responsible for their fashion sense beginning today."

"It is an honor, my dear friend. Come in!"

The four Kristovas found themselves at a greenhouse after the quick walk at Lili Crossman's gardens. Inside the greenhouse was her tulip blocks and her newly collected butterflies. Katarin was amazed by the tulips while Antonia was stunned by the species of butterflies. All were unique and costly.

"You don't have plans to marry, do you?" Madam Kristova was not the only woman in the capital who had decided to become a spinster.

"I want to follow your footsteps. Besides, I found none to like. Everyone is either for money or beauty."

"But, Lili, you are beautiful."

"You always say that, but the scar on my face tells me otherwise."

Madam Kristova gave Madam Crossman a grip on her arm and hugged her tight. Even if she had that awful scar on her face, she was a good person and a talented one. The scar did not make her less of a being, or less of a woman. And she deserved all the love from anyone. Madam Kristova and she had been friends the moment they met in the capital. And both had been keeping in touch for years, helping and caring for each other through the exchange of letters after Madam Kristova shunned anyone she knew.

"Did Diana write to you?" inquired Madam Crossman.

"She did, right after Tristan's death. She asked for reconciliation and I gave it. I cannot blame her. Society had been trying to cripple everyone till this very day. I can't blame her for taking the other side."

"That's true. And Isabel wrote to me, too. Just recently. She tried to make amends. And she promised I will have more clients for the Queen's Ball this year."

"And? Have you forgiven her?"

"I think I should. If God forgives, how can I not?" But Maria frowned at her friend's notion and forced herself to remain silent.

"What about you and Edward?" Madam Crossman asked the wrong question this time.

"We have no hope. The source of my hate for him will never run dry."

"Just like your love for him." Lili Crossman spoke as if she was certain of Maria's sentiments. But being the latter's intimate fellow, she was aware. Though Madam Kristova had a lot to say about the man, she kept her silence again.

"But I can guarantee that he loved you deeply, Mary."

"I know he did," Maria admitted, "he just couldn't. He loved me but it was not enough for him to choose me."

"Does that mean all those years you are just upset because he never chose you?"

"I would have accepted if he did not choose me, because it was for Tristan's sake. But he blamed me for his death too. That was the worst misfortune I ever received in Hert."

"Because you blamed him first."

"Who wouldn't? He loved his dear cousin more than anyone, and he just let him die. What a disgrace!"

"Must you hate him until now? It's been twenty years, Mary."

"Everything is still vivid. I cannot let it all go. Tristan was very dear to me, Lili. You know that."

"I am sorry, Mary. Edward and you became very close fellows of mine. And I hope you will resolve the bad blood between you two already."

"You can keep on hoping, Lili. Just don't expect anything from me."

"Of course."

When the Kristovas settled at a bench to talk about the Queen's Ball with Lili, Antonia stayed at the greenhouse to study Madam Crossman's butterflies. She was eager to make a poem out of it. Yet when she tried to look closely, all of the butterflies flew and surrounded her as if she was one of them.

Elric Coldwell, with a hat to hide his face, passed by the greenhouse after he was sent for an errand by his uncle at Lili Crossman's boutique, and felt something strange when he saw someone among the butterflies of the said madam. No one was ever allowed inside that heaven but the ones who were close to the collector alone. That made him curious all the more. For that reason, he slowly walked towards the greenhouse to learn about the trespasser.

At first, he thought the person was a man because of the pants, but it turned out to be a woman when her hat fell on the ground, revealing her bloody hair. The closer he went near her the sooner he realized she was the same maidservant at Kristova Mansion. That made him retreat, for he must avoid her at all cost. But the sight made him moonstruck that he could never forget the woman's face, the face which had already begun haunting his thoughts for many days since their awful encounter. And her eyes, her eyes were so gentle despite the anger she had shown him that night.

Chapter Five

From all the avoiding that Elric did towards the Kristova Mansion, he stumbled onto them unknowingly one inevitable day at the West Mansion when he visited Wilfred. He was there to discuss some matters with his comrade regarding his Uncle Edward.

It was not really intentional but Madam Kristova suddenly changed her plans for that day and allowed Juliet and the twins to pay their respects to the Wests. And with that, the three adorned the West Mansion.

Master William and Madam Morgana, Juliet's parents, were the gladdest that day in the capital to have finally met their granddaughters which they had never imagined to ever take a sight of. You see, when Juliet eloped with Rudolf, the West family disowned her. Yet all of them had enough of the bitterness and of being upset against each other. After everything they all still had the same blood flowing in their veins.

"You know, Elric? You do not owe your uncle everything," Wilfred said to his comrade that day. "We can say he has been a good uncle to you but that does not mean he owns you. Even love cannot give you the right to own your person."

"I know. And I am with you on that. It is just I cannot help myself thinking I must give back to him, in any way, like I should follow what he wishes me to. Without him, I'd be nothing."

"Must that be the only way, Elric?"

"I cannot think of anything."

"Of course, you will. You are Elric, the most sensible one in our group."

Their attention was taken by a commotion in the living room of the house. Wilfred asked a maidservant about the cause of it when she passed by and she told him that one of his sisters arrived. He was then excited to relay the details. "Elric, have you heard?"

"I did. And I am leaving," Elric, who was beside a window, replied after taking his coat with him for exit.

"Why?"

"You know why."

"If you retreat like that every time a woman appears, you are never going to be a married man," Wilfred teased.

"I am just trying to be a good nephew. Besides, I am not a member of your family to join such a reunion. And please, next time you visit me." Elric was expected to have such a reaction because his uncle always showed hatred towards Wilfred's other sister, Isabel, who had lived outside the West Mansion already. Not to mention she once tried her charms toward the young Coldwell.

"Fine, fine. I will. You can take your exit now."

Everything was well when Elric left Wilfred at the study but when he took his exit at the back door of West Mansion to hide himself from Isabel, things escalated from bad to worse. One, he met Katarin, whom he thought was Antonia, which he did not know the name and real identity yet. He looked at her fiercely, but the woman only bowed to his presence and walked past him, almost running. "Mama will kill you if you won't get inside this instant," she called.

Elric then thought of her voice to be different even though the face looked the same with the maidservant he met beforehand. So, he went on his way baffled until another lady who looked just like the one he saw earlier bumped into him. She was running fast and her dress was ragged.

"What is wrong with you this time?!" Antonia panted as she angrily asked Elric. "And why are you always everywhere?"

"But—" he stuttered. He saw her a moment ago and now there she was again. "You truly are a witch, are you not?"

"Being a redhead doesn't make me one, mister!" That was when Elric noticed. The lady he was staring at was a redhead while the one who went inside the house was raven-haired.

"Then how did you change your look in an instant?"

"Why are you even insisting that I have capabilities to do such a thing? I am no witch!"

"If the devil cannot reach you he will send you a witch."

"So be it! But I will have you instead, as my familiar, for naming my sins." Antonia wickedly laughed before she left him.

He turned to her. "Why are you here by the way?"

"It's none of your concern, unkind sir. Go home or I'll put a spell on you."

Elric was smiling as he walked himself out of the West domain. The woman was brash and bold. And she made him burn as if she was the oxygen he needed for fire to appear.

"That means you can work with your Aunt Isabel, Katarin," was what Antonia heard from Madam Morgana, their grandmother, when she entered the drawing room.

"I hope to never disappoint her if given the chance." Katarin gave a weak smile though she was pretty excited inside.

"And this is Antonia, mother," Wilfred introduced the other Kristova twin.

"Oh, my! They are nothing but the same, are they not?" Master William was astonished.

"Darling, that is what a twin means," Madam Morgana smiled, shyly.

"But look at them! If Antonia is not a redhead, they'd be exactly one person. It's something you do not see every day, Morgana. Even the Lockehart twins could not match."

"Whatever you say, William."

"Papa is right, mama," retorted Wilfred on the side.

"Ugh, men!"

The three Kristovas were required to have a meal with the Wests that night, too. Isabel joined the group and some buried stories became known to those who were unaware.

"Oh, girls! Your mother was a very willed lady back then," Isabel began. "Did you know that she eloped with your father?"

The twins did not reply and were never surprised at such truth. Wilfred, however, felt Isabel's disrespect towards the beloved guests. Juliet remained a spectator to her eldest sister's rage and felt sorry for her. She was the most affected by the family's crooked upbringing because she was too filial and was afraid to stand on her own.

"If she never did that, we would have never met these lovely girls, would we, sister?" Wilfred fired. "Do not be so sad still, for not being the prettiest in the country. You don't have to be when you are already. Besides, the character would make a person love the other being more than anything."

"Tell that to their great-aunt," Isabel answered Wilfred but turned to the twin sisters.

"I do not like where your conversation is heading," Master William warned. "Both of you, stop."

"However, I am blissful to have met you here tonight. After Madam Kristova sent a letter for the Queen's Ball, I have been very excited," Isabel mentioned. "Are you?"

Katarin and Antonia answered "Yes" and "No" respectively at the same time which surprised everyone, even Juliet. As a mother, Juliet didn't know Antonia would be that way. Maybe it was because she was closer to her father than her mother.

"Why not, my dear Antonia?" asked Wilfred.

"I am not good at dancing," she answered, which left everyone laughing except for Katarin. And as an affectionate sister, Katarin held Antonia's left arm, tightly, to make her feel she was on her side. Only the twins knew it was not really because of such a reason, but out of Antonia's hate regarding those events which would require her to look pretty. And she did not, even once, dream to look more than what she was. She despised pretenses and vanity. She just wanted to be real, the real her.

"Don't worry, dear. I am sure Madam Kristova already had a solution for such a tribulation," Isabel revealed, for it took one to know one. Maybe Maria even completed the whole alphabet for her plans too, Isabel thought. The woman was always ahead of her. Already a brute before she could decide to be barbaric.

"Unsympathetic, don't you think?" Antonia thought, but said her words out loud.

"What?" Isabel replied with awe.

"For Hert to think of dancing when Ardia is facing war, and Primus being left with no fathers because all died in battle."

Everyone left speechless at the thought. No one talked for the rest of the evening meal and the night ended after all of them finished drinking wine while listening to Wilfred play the pianoforte in the drawing room. Good bye hugs and kisses were given before the three Kristovas headed home.

"Mother, have you regretted marrying papa?" Katarin asked Juliet the moment they were inside Madam Kristova's carriage.

"No," she replied without a doubt. "Your father was the kindest. He promised no stars and everything but to choose me every day the moment I choose him. Back then, the capital was too much. Aunt Maria knows that. And your father gave the solace I longed for years. Though I was very young at the time, I was betrothed already. That was why I wanted to run. My family was like the other families in Hert, cruel to their children, the daughters particularly. And I was fortunate to find a man like your father. We created a family and though we were not wealthy, the love we have was rich enough to sustain us for years."

That night Katarin wished she would have the same story. Meeting a man with such a heart would be huge and grand, for every woman's dream at that age was to marry a man whom she loved and would be willing to return it in the same amount. Perhaps more.

Though Antonia liked that, to be loved deeply, she never wanted to get married or find a man. Such notions always meant settling and having restrictions. And restrictions would be best defined as one could never easily do whatever she wanted because another being's permission would be a requirement. Yet as she was looking at the moon, she thought of Elric, the man whom she did not know the name of, only from what house he was from. The man who made her smile just by remembering how he thought she was a real witch and a maidservant, too. Though he seemed someone she would not hesitate to kill, he was a mystery who was worth her time just to be unveiled.

"But why does wanting to kill someone feel like wanting to tame them?" Antonia whispered in her mind. "And why do I think of him and not papa? What is he to me now?"

Chapter Six

Two weeks before the Queen's Ball, three fellows agreed to gather again. That time they met at a park to be able to concentrate on anything they'd wish to tackle. In addition, no one would be around to hear any of their plans.

Elric Coldwell, the successor of Coldwell Mansion, was the first one to arrive. His father, Captain Stewart Coldwell, was a great man who died in war and was a receiver of many awards after his death. But what could gold medals do for a son who lost his father at an early age? His mother, Cruelle Silverson, followed her husband a year after. But before she left, she showered her son all the love she had to make him the man he must become. So, Elric was left under his uncle's care and was the sole heir of Coldwell Mansion, for Edward Coldwell was the firstborn and had neither family nor children. From then on, Elric felt obliged, too, to be what his uncle wished him to be, even if that meant doing things he never imagined doing.

Richard Kovalski arrived next. He was from a family of merchants. His family had been trying to climb the elite status for decades but never succeeded. And now, it's Richard's responsibility to achieve the dream his family never realized in the past. That's why he was so eager to meet and marry any woman from the elite class since it was the fastest way. Engaging in any form of business would take him years to do so, unless it's illegal. His friends knew his situation and had been helping him, but he just seemed so lost that he never got to focus on a single woman alone. He acted as if he was responsible to love every broken heart he met. But he, too, was charming himself. If he was not, women would never dare give him their attention. For who would love a man who knew nothing about loving only one woman and whose main aim was to accumulate wealth in his relations? No one.

The last to arrive was Wilfred West. He proved to the first two that he was the king of all lazy bones. Wilfred was the sole living son of West Mansion and was nearing thirty summers. His older brother gave up his heirship for love, travel and war, making him the last man on the lineage to carry everything that must be carried. He, too, like Richard, had his share of women, and was unlike Elric who remained faithful to someone he never yet encountered. William West, his father, became a cripple from an illness they did not know at the time. And his mother, Morgana Locke, never left his father's side after everything. And this made Wilfred pray to meet a loyal woman just like his mother, because such a woman would help a man achieve his dreams. But his quests were all a failure.

"Gentlemen, I need your help." Wilfred was downhearted when he asked his comrades that day. He had been thinking about his nieces since he met his older sister. "It's about my dear nieces."

Richard asked, "What can we do?" while Elric kept silent about it, thinking if he's even qualified for the proposition. They were Kristovas to begin with.

"I am worried about them. Once they are declared to the public, every man will seek their attention. And I neither want them to settle for people like me nor Richard, no offense."

"None taken," smiled Richard who was guilty of his comrade's judgement.

"You see, they deserve everything in the world, a good house and a man with a loyal heart. Just like you, Elric."

Yet Elric interrupted, "I cannot believe you have this in mind when the war is coming our way. No one would prefer marrying in a state of calamity."

"You are right, Elric. But some will do everything to find solace and diversion. And I do not want my Katarin and Antonia to be just lovers for a night. They deserve a man's lifetime."

"Yet what I am worried about is why they cannot decide that for themselves." Elric never liked the idea of people being boxed and lives being written by others because he, too, was and still a victim of such but willingly conceded to it out of gratitude. He craved and was craving for freedom.

"Are you saying I am authoritative?"

"You can think whatever you like, Wil."

"You're right. They can choose whomever they wish to marry and even the life they pray for, but we must not let them fall for fools."

"Thank you for thinking highly of me. But still, Edward Coldwell will kill me if he knows that his dearest nephew is helping a Kristova."

"Make that Kristovas," Wilfred corrected.

Yet Richard suggested, "I bet he won't. You're his only successor. What if this will bring change to the two houses instead?"

"One can dream, of course," Elric murmured. "Still, it's too risky for my part."

"Then you can be the whisperer whatsoever. You will be telling people things which will make them avoid my nieces."

"That seems fine," agreed Richard.

"Agreed," Elric confirmed.

"I owe you this one, Elric and Richard. Thank you!"

"That's what comradery is for." Richard tapped Wilfred's shoulder.

After the meeting, Richard and Elric headed towards the library. While doing so, Richard kept asking his comrade about the Kristova Mansion.

"What was it like inside?"

"Haunted."

"You are jesting! If father did not call for me I would have been there. What about Madam Kristova? How did she look?"

"A woman," Elric answered again, apathetically, in a few words.

"Elric! You are so greedy. Give me details." Richard seemed irritated. "Descriptions, more adjectives, and complete sentences."

"There is nothing to give."

"Have you seen Wilfred's nieces?"

"They were the type someone like us must be running away from." Though he never saw them as he presumed, Wilfred warned them about the two.

"Really?"

Elric amused himself by giving Richard information that would mean negatively if over-analyzed. "Really."

"But I agreed to help Wilfred. Will this ruin my image?"

"Is there anything more to ruin?"

"Elric!"

"Don't worry. It's not something like that, my friend."

"Good." Richard was relieved. "However, I must part ways with you at the moment. I cannot seem to take your terrible jesting any longer."

"You are just saying that. I bet you'll be womanizing again," Elric whispered.

"Just ask me if you want to learn. I will teach you for free."

"I am afraid I have to pass. I'm loyal to only one."

"As if there is one," was what Elric heard from Richard before they completely separated ways. He just smiled at his comrade's retort and thought there was actually one, an untamable one to be specific.

Elric then went on his way to the library. He received a message yesterday from the librarian about new international books arriving that day. The library was one of his favorite places in the capital. The books were aplenty, the place was silent, and only a few were frequenting it. It was perfect for him who kept on avoiding inevitable meetings and conversations from people he never wished to talk with.

The librarian greeted him with a smile. "Mr Coldwell, the storeroom is yours for the day. I assure you."

"Thank you, Miss Noir."

"My pleasure, sir."

He entered the storeroom and settled there for the whole afternoon. He felt he was in heaven at the scene. The stock of books became towers around him. He read and read and read until he fell asleep. And in his dream, he saw the woman again with hair in flames and was glaring at him.

Elric awoke and was glad he did but felt his sweat dripping from his temples. He could not believe it. He was dreaming of her again, making him more confused about his heart. What baffled him was the thought that whatever he was feeling was not suffocating. He was rather curious about the woman. He wanted to touch her like how a gardener did to the leaves of the shrubbery he was nurturing, or how a tailor palmed the fabrics he decided to make a suit of. He wanted to feel if her cheek was warm like the first ray of the sun during the break of dawn in spring or if it was cold as the first snow in winter. And he wanted to cup her hand as if he was enveloping a hot coffee on an autumn morning. He did not want to deny it, she mattered to him. Her simple act of kindness without touching his skin reached his core. He did not want to admit it but he could not lie to himself, she grew on him.

He only went back to his senses when someone was trying to open the door of his heaven. It was supposed to be his for the day. He stood to lock it but before he could reach the door a woman in a man's clothing appeared and went inside the room.

"This room is mine for the day, young lady," he growled. "What do you want?"

"Not you, of course. Move away!" she said after hearing ladies murmuring behind the door and pushed Elric aside. Though she knew who she encountered that instant, evading the ladies was more important than avoiding or killing the man she just saw.

Elric then closed the door as if a thunder struck on them which made the ladies left the area as it was clear from the fading sound of their pounding shoes on the library floor. "Why were they after you?" he asked. "What did you do?"

"Maybe I looked familiar. A former lover perhaps." Antonia assured herself to stand far from the man she was in the room with. He seemed to have not discovered who she was. Though she could not help having a conversation with him, he was making her desire to get to know him herself, forgetting what she was told about him.

"Do you think they believed your disguise?" Elric couldn't help himself figuring out the person in front of him as a lady, the very same woman he was dreaming earlier, the maidservant he first encountered at Kristova Mansion in the flesh. And he felt the same desire, to learn who she was that he could not stop himself from having a talk with her. He couldn't just let the opportunity go. He had been wanting to ask her why she needed to look like a man and even why she was working at Kristova Mansion.

"Do I not look like one?"

"You look rubbish with your theater costume. Who are you playing? A madwoman in a man's clothing?" Antonia was not aware she was humoring Elric at the same time and took it as an offense.

"Oh, yeah?" Antonia stood appalled by the Coldwell's honest comment. "Do you want to see a real madwoman then?"

"Just save it. Tell me, why are you not at Kristova Mansion at this very moment?"

"But how did you know it was me?" Antonia thought he knew her as Madam Kristova's granddaughter, but she was wrong. She was still the maidservant to him.

"Who are you fooling? And if you want to be a man, that's not the wardrobe for you." He saw her two times wearing man's clothes and assumed she was trying to escape the mansion. Maybe because the madam of the house overlabored her or maybe she was just insane and was fond of troublemaking.

"Follow me," Elric said. He wanted to help her and his reason was to be on good terms with her. He wished for him to be familiar with each other, and more, be friends with her. The lady seemed harmless despite the madness she was emitting.

Antonia Kristova followed Elric Coldwell without a slight of doubt until they entered the backdoor of what seemed to be a theater. They found themselves in a room full of clothes for men and women in different ranks and costumes, which were out of this world and found only in books. The latter chose the clothes for the former to wear before he left the room for her to change. And between the walking and picking of clothes, their conversation was solely through glances and gestures which were full of naughtiness and jesting, as if they were children again.

"Tell me, Mr Coldwell. What's with the sudden change of disposition towards me?" Antonia asked when she exited the room for Elric to see his work. He made her confused, because he was pretty angry and mean during their past meetings. He was not like whatever he was showing this time, calm and soft.

"Because you are a person too," Elric admitted. "And forgive me for my manners the first time we met, even on the next."

He circled Antonia and noticed her hair was unruly at the back of her neck. "Can I touch you?" He sounded wavering.

"What?" she crimsoned, but he did not notice.

"Your hair needs to be properly tucked inside your hat."

Antonia laughed as she nodded. Elric removed her hat before he arranged her hair and coiled it. As he put the hat back again, she murmured her gratitude. "Do you have a fever?" he inquired after he accidentally brushed a finger on the side of her neck. She was not cold as snow or warm as the sun's ray when he palmed her cheek, she was burning like a hearth on a summer evening in the middle of a cold desert. She denied and backed away.

"Is that it?" Antonia looked like a noble gentleman now, handsome and knowledgeable. "You see me as a person."

"There is more, indeed, but I am afraid the rest of it will remain a secret as long as it is not yet confirmed." Elric agreed with his senses to know about what he was truly feeling towards the lady he was with before he gave away information that would either bring his heart harm or bliss. "As of the moment, the advice I can give you is to trust nobody."

"Even you?"

He nodded. "Even me."

"I don't understand."

"Let us say you're just too trusting."

"Partly, yes. But I believe mistrust is earned and not the other way around. I think trust is the normal thing we give people at first. Mistrust, later."

"I get your point, but I want you to promise me."

"Promise what?"

"That this will be the last time you will dress as a boy, or a man, or anything not of your gender."

"Why?" She mused, "It is fun. And fun is my middle name."

"It is fun, but it can endanger you when it is not your fortunate day or when your guardian angels are asleep."

"Do not dare say you are a fortuneteller or a reader of stars because you do not look like one. Are you an astrologer though?"

"I am not, of course. But you know what I am trying to say."

"But you insisted that I am a witch. And witches fear no one but themselves."

"Cut it out. You are no witch. I know that now."

"How?"

He smirked. "Because witches are cold, and you are not."

"But you cannot tell me what to do or not do. I am my own master."

"I am aware of that. I just want to make sure you are safe," was what Elric admitted which made Antonia look at him intently, in the eyes and noticed kindness in them.

"Well, then. Promise me, too," she murmured.

"Promise what?"

"To let me be a man when we're together."

Elric drew a dashing smile, as if he was a man deeply in love. "Why?"

"I feel safe in your company. I was told never to be in the same room with you, but I am much inclined, as I imagine, to be on your side in a sea of people." Antonia's honesty made the man before her almost cry. It was beautiful to hear that someone felt safe with you, that you were not a threat but someone that another being could stand beside with.

"But we can never meet again under this kind of circumstance. We were born to avoid each other." Elric cleared his throat, not allowing himself to shed a tear in front of the woman nor hug her tight even. He should not. It would be cruel to ask for someone to hold you when you could not hold them forever.

"I understand what you mean," said Antonia with eyes focused on the wooden floor, thinking it was because she's a Kristova. But to Elric it was because, in his head, she was just a servant and his uncle hated that kind of standing for a woman to have emotional connections with. The old man was sure that the friendship between a man and a woman would lead to romance, and he warned his nephew for that eventuality to be a grave mistake, something forbidden and not allowed.

"So, is this the moment we separate ways?" asked Elric when silence took its place between the two of them.

"Is it all right for me to never return the clothes?"

Elric only nodded and earned a farewell from Antonia after, which he did not attempt to return. Seeing her go made him wish he was not from an elite class nor from a wealthy family. Maybe that way he could have a chance to be friends with that lady who was not like the others he ever associated with. He promised himself it was the last time he got close to her. He prayed for it to be the last time being in the same room with her.

Chapter Seven

Katarin and Antonia received the training regarding balls, dances and social interactions as Madam Kristova planned. It was conducted one week prior to the Queen's Ball. It was an intensive one and Antonia hated everything about it. Katarin, on one hand, enjoyed every single bit.

"Oh, dear sister! Where's your source of enthusiasm over these things?" Antonia cried while lying on the floor after the last training session. Everything took place mostly in the drawing room.

"Why?" Katarin giggled while sitting beside her sister. "Do you want to take it?"

"No. I am just curious. You're amazing. You were never tired."

"Don't worry, poor thing. The ball is on Sunday. I'm sure it will be the last time you suffer."

"I disagree." Antonia was panting, her toes were painful and her knees were shaking.

"But why? Aren't you glad?"

"Aunt Maria told you, did she not?"

"Told me of what exactly?"

"Sending us to a training school," Antonia took a deep breath, "for two years."

"You mean, something like this for years?" Katarin was flabbergasted by what her sister revealed and was happy to hear it.

"You sound too excited, and you say it as if it will take a long time. I hate you, Kat."

"I'm sorry, Ant. These things are fun for me." The names Kat and Ant were what they used to tease each other when they were children.

"I know," was all Antonia could say then closed her eyes because she was too tired of the training.

On the day before the ball, the Kristovas went to the most expensive dress shop in the capital. Again. It was where almost all elite women got their dresses for important occasions. No dresses were alike. Each dress was the only one of its kind and design. That's why Madam Kristova became a regular despite the fact that its owner was her dear friend, Lili Crossman.

Katarin was so happy to see everything inside the shop. But Antonia was always Antonia. After trying one gown, she was already content. Even wearing a corset felt to her like a battle she always hoped to escape. "If only I'm a guy," she'd often say, "everything would not be too much to bear. Everything would be simpler."

However, Madam Kristova was a perfectionist and she never departed the place without feeling satisfied with the gowns her granddaughters tried on. And only after ten attempts of wearing those different heavy materials sufficed Madam Kristova's heart. She also bought a gown for her and Juliet before they left. It actually took them two hours, or three at most, to decide which was which. Katarin was all smiles while Antonia just had a sullen face.

When their group headed for a tea shop, Antonia asked permission to visit the library as it was quite close to where they were. Juliet granted her permission to do such but with Katarin's company. Katarin, however, begged to stay for tea, making Madam Kristova decide and let Antonia do what she preferred doing than getting bored with them three inside the tea shop while sipping who knew how many cups of tea.

"Isn't she too deviant?" Juliet murmured out of humiliation in front of Madam Kristova. But she did not hate her daughter the way she was or for the things she was fond of. Being the mother, she was just worried. The world would never be friendly to the weird ones. They would always be out of place or have no place at all.

"I don't agree with you, Juliet. Your daughter is just different from what was expected of her to become. Don't worry, she can manage herself. She's not irresponsible anymore as I have observed." Madam Kristova had been a keen looker and found improvements. Though Antonia needed all her eyes, she loved every part of her, the sane and the mad, as a grandmother would.

"I am a witness to that. She isn't sleeping anywhere she likes anymore. And she never loiters in the house with her sleeping garments, too." Katarin seconded Madam Kristova's observation.

"Maybe there's still hope," Juliet Kristova prayed before sipping her tea, but it was not for Antonia alone. She was aware Katarin loved witchcraft, too. And that was an abomination in the capital.

Richard Kovalski was with Elric Coldwell at the library to plan their strategy on "The Towering Project" as what the former decided to call it. Elric said it was a lame title but somehow went on with it to shun further discussion and debate. But sometime later, Mr Kovalski's attention diverted towards the entrance when an enchantress entered the building. The woman was wearing a black dress that wasn't revealing but surely showed the figures she tried hiding. Her red hair added much to her already striking form.

"Blimey! Who is that peach ready for plucking?" Richard was so astonished at the sight. And that's when Elric realized that the woman he thought of as a servant of Kristova Mansion was a Kristova blood herself.

"That, my friend, I think, is the other niece of your dear friend, Wilfred West," informed Elric after being moonstruck just like his fellow.

If Antonia wasn't wearing that expensive dress, Elric wouldn't know she was one of Wilfred's nieces. There was no judgement in that, but there was truth in it. Her dress was signifying Kristova air, its lavish style and dark color. It was a signature of Madam Kristova, not to mention the black poppy embroidery on the edges. If he hadn't been to Madam Lili Crossman's boutique, he would have never known such details. And he couldn't believe himself to realize it only now. The lady he thought of as a maidservant of Kristova Mansion was actually one of its new occupants, a pure Kristova.

"And let me remind you, she is out of our radar. So, shut your perverse mouth and keep your eyes and hands to yourself," Elric added.

"You're cruel, Elric. You said they were ugly."

"I never did." He shook his head. "You just presumed they were. And I thought I only saw Madam Kristova that night. This is madness! Besides, didn't Wilfred say men like you do not deserve a lady like her?"

"I can't run away from that beauty. I should be running towards it. Is she Katarin or Antonia?"

"I don't know, but I am certain you are hopeless. Wilfred will kill you, that is for sure."

"Well, she's worth dying. Look at her. Are you not spellbound? She's a redhead. For sure she can cast a spell on you."

"I know my limits, my dear friend. And I know how to control myself." Yet a mirage of defeat was visible to his view for he was aware at the moment that she had started to bewitch him long before he realized it.

"I hope you won't be able to control yourself after this day," Richard teased.

"And Richard," Elric added.

"What?"

"I think they are twins," he claimed after his mind went back to a memory of that day at the West Mansion.

"What?!"

Antonia Kristova passed by their table without giving a glance at Elric Coldwell, whom she had seen immediately when she entered the library. Maybe it was because she hoped she'd see him again and when she did, being a Kristova reminded her that they could never be anything but people who must avoid each other. Or in the worst and tragic possibility, adversaries.

Elric Coldwell tried all his best not to look at Antonia's direction when she settled somewhere visible to them. He never wanted to be so transparent to his fellow beside him. Call him pretentious, but to him he would always say he had full control over himself. But yes, he was glad to have met her first, even under a laughable circumstance.

Richard and Elric eventually devised a plan. Richard was blissful to know he would be escorting one of the sisters during the Queen's Ball for the whole evening as they had agreed. Elric decided to stay from afar and spread rumors about the two without being noticed.

When they were done discussing and Richard left him to clean the mess on their table, Elric glanced at Antonia only to find she wasn't there anymore. And he never understood why he found disappointment in that. He questioned himself, too. Which would have been better? Antonia, whom he did not confirm the name yet, being a maidservant or being a Kristova herself? And the answer was neither, for both were woeful options.

Antonia joined her family's tea party after her excursion at the capital's library. She was glad they waited for her for an hour but perplexed as well on how they managed to do it. Did they not bore themselves as time passed? What were they talking about for an hour? Though her mind was filled with those, she thought about the young Coldwell, whom she never had the bravery of asking about his first name because squabbling seemed to be a priority in every encounter. And even when they went home, Antonia remained preoccupied. She began thinking about why the Kristova and Coldwell Houses were against each other for years. She only heard stories and aftermaths from the maidservants but not its main cause.

"Antonia, love, are you feeling ill?" Madam Kristova was not able to stop herself from asking. She wasn't worried but was rather curious. What was in her darling Antonia's mind for her to look lost? What did she see in the library? What made her lonely? Her eyes were somehow gloomy as if dark clouds were looming.

"No, I am not. I am just tired from shopping and walking. Sorry for making you worry, Aunt Maria."

"I will have a maidservant bring you dinner upstairs. Proceed to your room right away."

"Thank you."

Antonia craved food while arranging her bed and was glad Katarin brought her what she wanted instead of the maidservants doing so. She badly needed someone to share her confusions with. And while eating, Antonia tried asking about the bad blood between Kristova and Coldwell, but Katarin knew nothing about it as well.

"Would you agree with me if I think it best to ask the madam of the house about it?"

"Do you hate my curious persona now, Kat?"

"No, Ant. Of course, not." Katarin was placing colorful stones at Antonia's bedside table. "I just believe she knows it more than anyone else in the house. She is the lead character of the story after all."

"And I thought you already hate me. But I agree with you. I should be asking her instead."

"That will never happen."

"What?"

"Me hating you, Ant."

"That's good to hear, Kat."

"And do not remove these stones," Katarin warned her sister. "They'll calm your nerves."

"Wine calms my nerves. Can you get me one?"

"Not tonight, Antonia. Not tonight."

Antonia enjoyed her food till she emptied all the plates. Katarin was happy to see that and before she left the room she hugged her sister as she said good night.

That night, Antonia prayed again. Yet she was surprised to hear her thoughts to have included the young Coldwell in her prayers. It wasn't much, but as a Kristova, she felt guilty of such an act.

That same evening, Elric and his uncle, Edward Coldwell, were in the drawing room and were trying to discuss the younger Coldwell's future. That was the kind of issue Elric was never fond of, for he knew he'd never be brave to stand his ground and choose something which was of his preference. Yet it's not something like him could ever avoid.

"Have you decided what to do with your life?"

"I'm still not certain, uncle." But he knew he wanted to be an artist. Someone who paints, particularly. He just never had the heart to tell him, for he once been told it was not practical and was merely an act of sluggishness.

"Do I have to choose the path for you?"

"No," he replied, though he knew very well his uncle chose on his behalf. "But I do wish you'll give me more time."

"Haven't I already?" was the question which cornered Elric, silencing him.

"I'll give you a year, but that can still change if something arises," Edward Coldwell informed his nephew.

"Of course, Uncle Edward."

Chapter Eight

The Queen's Ball came. It was the first ball during the season of the Great Nine, a nine-week long celebration of how Simetra thrived when the first war ended and to honor those who were heroes of the war. And like other masquerade balls the attendees were required to wear masks. It was said to be the grandest ball of the year in the capital, and everyone, either of noble rank or slave, was invited. As long as they could follow the theme, they could join the said event.

There would be dancing, tea parties, laughing, and of course, meeting new acquaintances and connections. The ball would start after the usual dinner time and would end at midnight. The main goal of the event was the public declaration of young ladies who were in the ages of twenty until five-and-twenty that year.

The Wests had been responsible for the ball due to their intimate relation with the former king. Isabel West became a spinster, a woman to them who did not marry at the age forty, just to organize the event which always took place at the Queen's Hall. And since the weather was on her side that year, she forcibly held it at the two-hectare park in the middle of the capital. However, it had been a talk for years, too, that if the matchmaker herself could not find her own husband, why would mothers entrust their daughters in her hands? Yet others believed that she had given up her own for other women to find their better halves, and with that, she was doing a great sacrifice for them in return.

All eyes were fixed at the red carpet when a group of four newcomers paraded themselves in. Everyone was aware of their dresses being designed by Lili Crossman, the capital's famous and expensive fashion designer. Though everyone wished to see the faces behind their masks, it was of no avail. But that never stopped them from staring and whispering magnificence to what they had seen. The group was then joined a little later by two men.

Wilfred West felt proud, as he always was, to join Madam Kristova's group of beauties for they were all strikingly beautiful in their own ways. Juliet Kristova was still the West Mansion's prettiest lady. Maria Kristova remained the capital's notable witch. And the Kristova twins were both wonderful that night. Wilfred believed to have gained friendship from Madam Kristova, which he owed to his nieces so much. And it was the friendship everyone would wish to have but afraid to ask due to the fear of being turned down. Or worse, being cursed.

Richard Kovalski was glad to meet the twin sisters in person. As expected, all of the women inside Kristova Mansion were splendid. He confirmed the redhead he saw in the library as Antonia and the one he would be escorting was Katarin. And he was certain that very moment for Elisa Pierce to have a resemblance with the two young ladies as well as with Madam Kristova.

After the commotion Elric Coldwell arrived with his uncle who decided to still join the ball after hearing Kristova Mansion's attendance after twenty years of its absence from the said event. Edward Coldwell was not fearful of the news, but he prayed to avoid unavoidable contact and exchange of toxic words with the woman whom he called a witch since time only both of them remembered. As they entered, Elric instantly noticed his dear friends and believed they were with the Kristovas. Madam Kristova was standing next to Juliet while Wilfred and Richard were at the opposite sides of the twins, enveloping them. And when his uncle conversed with the capital's well-known marketeer, Elric left his side immediately.

Maria Kristova from a distance, knew all too well who were standing beside Mr Ramini Qalif, the marketeer. The woman was Lili Crossman and the other was Edward Coldwell, the man who took from her three things— her best friend, her beloved and her heart. And that meant everything to be exact.

Edward Coldwell, after spotting his archenemy, escaped her sight. Seeing her made him heartsick but not angry. Guilty, too. And he accepted, like most days, that Maria Kristova would never grant him forgiveness. Who would? He gave her the name of a murderer when all she did was make a choice and free herself from a certain catastrophe. He believed there was no hope for them two. And even their grandchildren would suffer the same hatred from them if their paths would ever unite again.

"Tell me, Miss Kristova. Are you enjoying your stay in the capital?" Richard Kovalski asked the raven-haired on his side. She absolutely looked beguiling.

"I am. Ardia is only green while I see plenty of hues here." Katarin was savoring every moment she encountered in the capital.

"That is great. And this ball? Are you excited to be famous around Hert soon?" Richard, in some way, was calm that evening, not aggressive at all. And he was not into making Katarin, not Antonia, a prospect for his marriage plans. He was exhausted from his unethical endeavors and only wanted to see Elisa.

"I am not sure if I want to be the talk of every gathering. I do not want to give Aunt Maria any trouble."

"Why would you give her trouble?"

"I don't know. Perhaps for being me."

"Don't overthink much. That is bad for the brain, my dear."

Katarin only smiled at the thought. And to be honest, she was amused by Mr Kovalski's humorous nature. He seemed a fine man to her for her to wish to meet a prospect just like him in the future, agreeable and dignified.

Antonia whispered to her uncle, "Why is everyone staring at me? Am I analyzing things excessively? Do I look laughable?"

"Nonsense, my love. They are staring because they want to see the beautiful face behind your mask." Wilfred, who was eight years older than Antonia, was filled with pride to be standing beside the beauty he was accompanying.

"Am I attractive?" Antonia felt as if she was a clown with all her makeup and gown which to her was not just lavish but funny. She even thought of herself as a stuffed turkey on thanksgiving.

"A girl like you does not need to be told she's attractive when it's already obvious."

"I don't know. I actually wished to be a man."

"And for what reason?"

"You can do whatever you want. That's enough for me to dream of something unattainable."

Wilfred was taken aback. "That's what you think. Leaving for war is the last thing we men hope. Nobody wants to die. Do you?"

"If it is for the country, I'll never doubt doing it."

"Well, I wish I had your courage, my love," was the sincerest compliment he had ever given in all his years. He was never brave enough to die for anything. He blocked every path and opportunity leading to the garrisons. He even bribed captains and officers in the past just for him not to be called for a two-year military service which was supposed to be a requirement from the men in their country. He could only hope to be braver and manlier.

The main event of the ball transpired which demanded the ladies who'd debut to stand in the middle, forming a circle by facing each other and preparing for the dances. Thirty ladies gathered at the time, all with angelic attire except for two girls, Katarin Kristova, who wore the darkest night as if she was a black swan, and Antonia Kristova, who was wearing the bloody setting sun.

The first dance was all about greeting. The ladies would do it together like a flock of birds, waking asleep creatures in the morning light. Rumors were spreading, too, as they were dancing. Maria Kristova was full of pride to see her granddaughters blooming and becoming the ladies she wanted them to be. Graceful. Elegant. Being charmers spiced it all.

Elric, who was moving serenely at the crowd, heard people talking about Kristova Mansion. That it was a miracle the house finally attended the annual event. Some spoke of Madam Kristova's granddaughters being declared that night, too, and were of splendid beauty just like the madam herself.

When the first dance ended, the ladies took their masks off, leaving everyone with their jaws dropping especially when their eyes were enthralled by the two ladies of the same face and beauty, the ones who were wearing gowns in black and red. Their faces revealed Kristova Mansion and many, both ladies and gentlemen, went near them to get to know them. However, their interests betrayed them after some time. Telling people that they liked learning Witchery and drinking wine, respectively, were considered abnormalities. That was why after a few talks, the crowd left them. And Elric, he did not need to spread rumors about the two because they both did it for him. His part was accomplished with no efforts rendered at all.

For the second dance, the ladies were required to have a partner, gentlemen with masks still, but not of the same blood or house. Richard Kovalski immediately partnered with Katarin Kristova as planned. Unfortunately, Wilfred West needed to partner with another lady, leaving Antonia Kristova to dance alone if no one would stand before her in time. Even so, Antonia was still confident to dance without somebody. She even preferred to have nobody at all.

Both Wilfred and Richard were glad when Elric stepped up and saved Antonia from further pity given by the surrounding crowd. Wearing a mask made him a mystery to Antonia who in return appreciated his guts to dance with her. Yet at the time, he was feeling drunk though he did not taste any drop of intoxicating liquid, for he knew that she was the girl he must avoid but just could not. His heart would not let him and his emotions were chaotic. He was happy and uneasy. Still, he danced handsomely as expected from him by everybody.

"May I know your name?" Antonia asked.

"Men should ask the name first and not the other way around. Nevertheless, the name is Elric."

"I disagree with you, Elric. If one has a voice, one must never fear to ask," Antonia answered, making Elric smirk.

"And you are named?"

"Antonia."

"What a lovely name, just like herself," he said to himself.

Antonia Kristova and Elric Coldwell felt more than content while dancing and even when it ended. They were, as books say, over the clouds without wanting to come down. But things would end as well as dances. When Elric bowed, Antonia curtsied.

"Your voice seemed so familiar. From what house are you, sir?" Antonia asked again, but was answered by Elric's taking of his mask off his face which turned her face red. "Mr Coldwell! Haven't we agreed we were born to avoid each other?" She reminded both of them.

"Of course," was all Elric said as he slightly bowed his head and left Antonia standing in the middle of the crowd. Yet the name Antonia was engraved in his memory. And forever it would be etched there.

Both master and madam of mansions Coldwell and Kristova saw what transpired. The former was hopeful, but the latter felt bitter. So, they have decided to just leave the ball, taking with them their ward. Wilfred and his fellows did not expect that. And their plan for the night was ruined when the two groups met at the entrance of the park with Wilfred and Richard tailing the Kristovas.

"Madam Kristova, it's good to see you after many years of hiding," Edward Coldwell greeted and with him was his nephew who was standing behind him, trying to avoid eye contact with the women in front of them.

"The feeling isn't mutual, Mr Coldwell. And I wasn't hiding," answered Madam Kristova with disinclination in every word she uttered. "I was meditating."

"Meditating from what?"

Maria smiled. "From murdering you in public."

"You still hate me," Edward teased.

"I am glad it is transparent enough for you to see. I hope we won't meet each other again after this very unavoidable occasion, Mr Coldwell, even in the afterlife."

"And here I thought to see you again in hell."

"Pity, for you to still be obsessed with me."

Maria Kristova did not wait for Edward Coldwell's retort and started walking outside the park. Juliet West followed the madam with her daughters Katarin, who waved good bye to his uncle and his friend, and Antonia, who only glanced at Elric with regretful eyes. Maria's carriage appeared and took them home

Before Elric headed for home, he calmed his mind by walking along Apollo River alone. He did this a lot in the past when everything was too overwhelming. And he had so much to think over after the encounter between his uncle and Madam Kristova. He wanted to be friends with Antonia before he knew she was Antonia. And he was not giving that up. So he then made some plans. However, all became futile when he arrived home late that night.

He found his uncle in the living room, and he was certain the man was waiting for his return. "Elric," Edward broke the silence, "you'll be leaving next week for the garrison."

Elric, unlike Wilfred, was never afraid to offer service in the military. Yet reading between the lines, he figured his uncle was sending him to avoid the Kristovas. And he did not ask his uncle to confirm his suspicion. He just knew.

"You'll be sent to the North," Edward added which Elric taken by surprise. Maybe the blood feud between the two houses was greater than he expected for him to be delivered to the most difficult garrison in the country.

"Is there anything else?"

Edward Coldwell stared at his nephew for a few seconds before saying, "If you have any interest towards that girl, I'm afraid you must leave this house. And if you still want to be my successor, find another lady. I'll give you two years to make up your mind."

"I understand," said Elric before leaving the room with a sorrowful heart.

But the uncle knew that his nephew's heart was unlike his. Elric grew up to be the kind of man who knew what he wanted after dealing with his mind. He stood to his decisions and was willing to be corrected. Edward was afraid for Elric to be heartbroken after loving a Kristova. It happened to him, and he was not able to come to the surface even after twenty years. He kept drowning.

That night, too, Madam Kristova was agitated. She couldn't sleep, and she wanted to lash out. To control her anger, she kept walking inside the house from the first floor to the last one. She must protect her babies. She must send both Katarin and Antonia to the training school. Two years would be enough. And by the time they were out, Antonia, particularly, would have forgotten about the young Coldwell.

Antonia awakened because of the noises she heard outside her room. She never feared ghosts and was even motivated to see at least one of them. To her curiosity, she went outside and saw her great-aunt walking here and there while murmuring. Antonia agreed with herself that her aunt was still distressed by Sir Edward Coldwell. Yet now, Elric and she added to the picture. Maybe she did fail to hide her fondness for the young man. But he was just worth befriending. Something about him was pulling her close to him like the moons to their respective planets. But unlike the moons, the more she would try to pull away, the more she would be dragged towards him. Then perhaps they would make a collision.

And everyone knew what would happen next after every collision, both would be in ruins. Still, Antonia believed he was worth that risk.

Chapter Nine

Friday it was when Katarin and Antonia asked their mother to take a walk. They were fortunate she was in the mood to let them go that morning without saying a word. So, they left the house quickly before she changed her mind. They were dressed in beautiful garments which made the walkers eye them from time to time.

Antonia insisted on going to the library while Katarin decided to go to a tea shop. Since they never agreed with each other's likings, they settled for separating ways. And within two hours, they must meet again at the place where they parted.

Katarin was enjoying her tea and own company when a woman approached her. She was wearing a fine dress and seemed like an angel to Katarin's view. "Can I join you, miss? You look lonely being alone and all," she said.

"But I am not lonely."

"Is that a no?"

"Yes," Katarin smiled. "I mean, do join me."

"I've seen you at the Queen's Ball. You were enchanting."

"Thank you, Miss—?"

"Pierce," the woman continued. "The name is Elisa Pierce."

"I am Katarin."

"Katarin Kristova, I know. I saw you with Madam Maria that night."

"Oh, I see. You were there too."

"What are your interests, Miss Kristova? Hobbies?"

"Haven't you heard? I'm a house person."

"What do you mean by a house person?"

"I'm pretty average. I like sewing, cooking, cleaning, and doing household affairs for the family."

"Those are chores. Not hobbies. And no, you're not average. You're beyond that, a miracle perhaps." Elisa's eyes had dark shades under. She looked tired and dejected. "I don't like doing those. I prefer going out, which makes me an outside person then."

"You're funny, Miss Pierce."

"So are you, Miss Kristova."

Elisa groaned after sipping her hot chocolate. "This is my favorite in this shop. It is so refreshing. And I need sugar for more energy. I need it as an outside person."

"What's an outside person like?"

"Well, I am a lady escort. Others call me names like prostitute and all, but I just tour people around. I love talking and making people laugh, purely entertaining them."

"A prostitute? That is horrible. Are you fine hearing that from them?"

"I got used to it. Besides, it is not the truth. I am content with my truth."

"Is there any way I can help?"

"No. I promise you, I am the last person you must engage with. You will be hated by people."

"I am not afraid of that. What I fear is my great-aunt's reputation being tainted by my deeds."

"She's your grandmother. Of course, you'll feel that way."

"And I think I just did ruin her image. I told everyone at the ball that I have an interest in Witchery."

"I heard that one. But I am no judge. And your grandmother is neither. Besides, her image is already formidable enough before your arrival. Don't worry so much."

"Why do you speak as if you know her very well?"

"She's Madam Kristova, the most famous spinster Hert ever has. She was the one labeled as a witch for being into Alchemy. Yet she is a giver, too. Two beings in one body."

"She's amazing, is she not?"

"Indeed!" winked Elisa. "Anyway, thank you for your time. I enjoyed it. See you around, Miss Kristova."

"And thanks to you too." Katarin was happy to have met a new friend. Her demeanor was reassuring, like family.

Antonia, on the other side, found joy again in books. That time, she was reading about the planets and stars. And without her noticing Elric joined her table. When she felt him, she did not react nor say a thing.

"I despise our situation," Elric wrote in a paper with brows meeting after silence became unbearable. "Why must our relation be affected by the feud we did not witness?" He slid the paper to Antonia's view and the latter read it.

"I am not sure," Antonia thought and replied, "Maybe we are just good family members who strictly follow the rules."

Elric looked at Antonia after reading her reply and saw her mouthing the question, "Why do you ask?"

"I sincerely want to be friends with you, Miss Kristova," whispered Elric and he added, "even before I knew you were Madam Maria's relative," as he took the seat beside her.

"What do you see in me for taking such a risk? I am a drinker and not ladylike as you have said it," Antonia murmured to avoid attracting attention from the other five people in the library, including the librarian.

"That's it. You're different from the rest."

"Different? What am I, an otherworldly creature? That's a vague description, Mr Coldwell, is it not?"

"Is it? Then what word must I replace it with?"

"Dauntless, if that's what you mean."

"Then dauntless it is."

Both of them looked at the librarian when the old woman hushed them two. Antonia continued reading, but Elric asked again about her interests and things which she was passionate about. And she never imagined for him to be such a talker.

"This place is not for talking, sir," she grumbled. "And you will both get us kicked out from our houses if we are seen being friendly towards one another."

"Don't worry. The librarian is my person."

"Good for you, I guess."

"I'll wait for you in the storeroom."

"How sure are you that I will join you in there?"

"Then I'll keep on waiting till you meet me."

After thirty minutes Antonia appeared in the storeroom to meet Elric for the first time, not accidentally, but in a mutual decision. And if you would look at it, you'd say they were lovers who met in secret at a hidden place in the library. The gentleman seemed deeply in love, while the lady, though reserved, looked as if she was under a love spell. Unfortunately, both were just either in denial or naive with their feelings that they disguised them as wanting to be merely friends. But didn't they say that comradery was always the beginning of intimacy?

"If we can neither be friends nor more, what can we be?" Elric asked Antonia as soon as she was in sight. And he was very glad for the lady to join him.

"I am sure we cannot be cousins as well."

Elric laughed.

"Strangers with sincere concern for each other perhaps?"

"Are you familiar with the Greek classifications of love, Miss Kristova?"

"Yes, I am. And to which kind do you think we belong?"

"Agape."

"Ah, yes. The universal kind of love since it can be given to everyone."

"Exactly. Are we now settled?"

"Before everything, let's just remind ourselves that this meeting we currently have will eventually be forgotten and must not be shared with any other being alive or six feet below the ground."

"Of course, but I cannot promise to forget about it."

"Why is that so?"

"It is always good to reminisce, Miss Kristova. Memories make the soul alive."

"All right," Antonia sighed. "Since you've asked earlier, let's start from there. I like fencing, horseback riding, reading different kinds of books, writing anything, looking at maps and globes, eating, drinking and—"

"Sleeping."

"You remember."

"Why wouldn't I? I thought you were a servant that time. You looked like a madwoman."

"Madwoman." Antonia smirked. "I slept wherever I wanted when we first met, not to mention it was because of wine. My great-aunt corrected me the next day after hearing about our harsh encounter from the maidservants."

"At least something good happened out of it."

"Must I be grateful to you?" Antonia teased.

"No. Of course, not. But why do you have interest in things that will label you dauntless, by the way? And drinking, too."

Antonia then narrated they used to live in the countryside. They had vast plains there and vineyards. Her papa and she were pretty close and he treated her as if she were a lad. She was free growing up. And she never liked staying inside the house. Nature inspired her and kept her going. She was unlike her twin sister, who loved every household activity— the ones she called chores like sewing, cooking, cleaning and organizing the whole house, and whatnots. Also, Witchery.

She gave a smile. "Anyway, by the time Katarin is changing the curtains, the ones needed cleaning, they all turned into the sails of my ship made from my own bed. I know I'm skipping and not doing the essential stuff a female being must do, but my heart aches for the outside world. I long to travel places I have never been, live the lives of different people, and drink every wine in different countries. I want to explore, try things new and strange. I wish I could settle and feel content, but I want freedom."

"Your life is yours, Miss Kristova. You can do whatever you wish to do."

"Easy for you to say. You're a man. You're free to do whatever you want."

"Not in my case." Elric looked more serious this time. Somehow sad. "You see, life has its ways of making all of us feel trapped."

"What is your story?"

"Painting. I have always loved it since. I am not that good, but I am not bad either."

"What is wrong with painting? It's forever."

"My uncle thinks it is not practical, that it is just a waste of time and energy. And it's not a wise thing to do for a living. That is why all of my work is hidden from him."

"That's awful. But I do hope for him to accept every inch of you. Hiding who we truly are is a difficult thing to do."

"Indeed."

"Does that mean I will never get to see your works?" wondered Antonia.

"Probably."

"That is a tragedy."

"Is it?"

"A work of art not seeing the light is tragic. Like you."

Antonia earned a confusing stare from Elric. "Like me?"

"I know you hate being seen. But you must show who you truly are, the artist in you, and live freely as you wish to be."

"To be honest, I hate parties and gatherings. I do not even like talking much," he admitted after the long exchange they just had.

"Then why are we doing what we are doing now?" Antonia raised a brow at Elric, baffled at his revelation, as well as the fact that they were not even tired standing as they went through the whole conversation.

"It is because you are the one I am talking with. I feel accepted and understood. Is it not what people crave?"

"I believe it is, yes."

"Well, I am glad you have chosen me to share whatever you liked sharing with. No worries, I keep secrets and I don't judge people. I know I'll do the same when given the exact circumstance. We don't know people's stories and their storms. I always believed a person is like the sea. Complicated. Calm on the surface but plenty of movements under. And a different world lies within which is full of creatures weak and strong. We only know nothing."

"I agree with you. But, Coldwell, you must see the light."

"I do not need the light. You are enough for me. I need no more attention from the public when I know you exist."

Their interesting talk halted when a woman suddenly entered the storeroom. "What exactly on Earth are you two doing here?!"

"Talking?" Elric said as if he was caught stealing something.

"It's dusty around here." She noticed the lady beside the gentleman, "Katarin, is that you? Were you not in the tea shop when I left you?"

"Are you friends with my sister?" Antonia turned pale. What if they would be discovered by the master and madam of their houses?

"Oh, you are the twin sister. Katarin and I just conversed today at the tea shop. I don't know if you can count that as friendship. I am Elisa Pierce."

"It is nice to meet you, Miss Pierce. I am Antonia Kristova." Antonia shook hands with Elisa. "And if you may, I hope you have seen only dust."

"Is it because you're with the dust from the mansion of the enemy? Elric, isn't it?"

"Yes, nice to meet you. You're the lady escort, I believe." He shook hands with her too.

"I am."

"Richard Kovalski talked about you once or twice."

"Only once or twice? Pity! Anyway, I'll go ahead. I thought this was the water closet. And yes, I only saw dust." Elisa ran along, leaving Antonia and Elric staring at each other.

"Can we meet here again? Tomorrow?" Elric asked before they said their good byes.

"Same time?"

"Yes."

"I won't promise, but we'll see."

"That is enough for me. And before we go, can I call you by your first name?"

"Yes, Elric, you can."

Chapter Ten

On the next day, Saturday, Antonia snuck out of Kristova Mansion. Luckily, the women in the house did not ask of her since it was a day for their cleaning and she hated doing so. She did not get out wearing a dress though. She was in a man's garments again.

"Antonia?" Elric asked in confusion when he saw a man's back as he went inside the storeroom that day.

"It's I, Antonio, kind sir!" Antonia faced him, smiling.

"Oh, it's theater day."

"They will be staying in for the whole day today. So, I have to do theater day. I hate staying in, it's boring."

"Forgive me if you have to do this, Antonia. I just feel like I'm running out of time."

"Why do you think so?"

"I will tell you soon."

"Alright. I guess you have your reasons for that." Antonia went to a pile of books and sat beside it, scanning whatever she found.

"What are your parents like, Antonia?" she heard Elric asking from behind.

"My mother is strict," she started, talking to the book in her hand. "She is pushing me off a cliff, you know, wanting me to be a proper lady. But I know it is for my own good. My father is soft but strong. He wants me to be brave every time. He says the world is hostile to the weak and weird, that I must be brave and confident. He taught me things a boy alone must learn, like fencing and all. Mama and he argued one night about my upbringing. Yet he insisted I have the choice to do what I want. I know fathers are controlling and authoritative, but he is from a different kind. I know mama thinks that I love father more than her. But do you not choose the ones who choose you?"

"Your mother only wants to protect you. Though it is in a way of hiding your true self."

"I hate a world filled with pretenses and people boxing others. It is too sad. Why are we here anyway if we cannot be our true selves?"

"But the world is what you have described it. And though we can be ourselves, we must be very mad or brave to do so and be willing to embrace everyone's judgment, without letting such judgments reduce us."

Silence passed them for a minute before Antonia asked the same thing to Elric. "What about your parents?"

"I don't know much about them. I was four when my father died and was orphaned when I was five. Mom died a year after my father's death."

"I am sorry, Elric," said Antonia, for opening wounds again which had difficulty healing through time.

"You did not know, do not be sorry. My father was in the military. And even as a kid, I knew that one day, he'd never come back alive. Growing up, Uncle Edward became my father figure. And my mother, she was the kindest. Though her heart was broken after father's death, she gave me the love a mother can offer her child. She actually left a journal which taught me a lot, like how to control my anger. That I should be understanding and not domineering. She wrote there that we all have different situations which greatly affect our decisions. Like how the rain nurtures flowers and storms drown them."

"She's a wise mother."

"She is."

"I'm sorry about your loss, Elric."

"It was difficult to accept, but that is life. People leave and there is nothing you can do about it but to accept with arms wide open."

"It's too complicated, I must say."

"Truly."

"By the way, Elric, do you know the root of the enmity between our houses?"

"I am glad you asked that, though I cannot give you the whole truth, only the things I have heard, or recalled."

"That's fine."

"Like other places, the houses in the capital combine connections and relations. So, a man from one house marries a woman from another. The Kovalskis and Coldwells did not avoid such a fate. What I know is that Uncle Edward had a cousin from the Kovalski family named Tristan, who became his favorite. They were inseparable. When Uncle Tristan began receiving education from a university he never failed visiting Uncle Edward with his best friend, a woman who was a Kristova."

"Aunt Maria?"

"Yes. And I don't know what was more to it but what happened next was horrible. Uncle Tristan died in his room. The detective discovered it was self-murder. He took poison. You see, he was studying Alchemy at the time and was teaching Madam Kristova about it to support his studies. We all know women cannot go to a university, that's why he was teaching her since she agreed to pay him for his teaching service. A minority believed he died because of his family's ambitious nature. But the Kovalskis blamed Madam Kristova, as well as Uncle Edward."

"What? Was she put into trial then?"

"She was not. There was no proof she did the crime. Only the public did the trial and hated her."

"Still, that was terrible."

"Maybe that's why she shunned the public. I believe she was devastated upon losing her best friend and being blamed in return for his demise."

"That is very tragic, Elric. I did not know. What I heard about Aunt Maria was that she left Ardia for the capital. She asked for her inheritance at a young age in exchange for her life here in Hert. I always looked up to her, you know. I still do. And she never failed to write us letters, too, telling us what this place looked like. She always seemed happy and full of life."

"She's really brave. No wonder she built the Kristova Mansion from the ground up even at a young age, she helped the house survive. She owned her life."

"Yes. But why do you think your uncle poisoned himself?"

"I don't know exactly. But for sure, he was in grief. Nobody does self-murder because of bliss."

"Of course, but what possibly could make a man sad to take his own life?"

"I am sure I don't wish to know."

"Does your friend Richard know? He is a Kovalski if I am not wrong."

"I didn't ask. His family is a mess until now."

They stayed quiet for some time, feeling the sorrow of that person they talked about and wondering if death cured his pain, praying for Richard to never do the same.

"Will you go to church tomorrow?" Elric suddenly thought because it would be a Sunday.

"Aunt Maria is not the religious type. But she has a god. She talks to him every night and when she's in distress. Maybe she will be there. And when she is, certainly I will be."

"I will expect that, and you, young man, must go home now. You have been here quite a while and you'll be hearing sermons for hours if you'll head home late for this day."

"I sure know about that. good bye, Elric."

"Good bye, Antonio."

"Right," Antonia laughed.

One afternoon a man and woman were meeting in secret. It happened in the garden of a monastery, twenty years ago. They were blaming each other about the death of their third member, who was the man's first cousin and the woman's best friend. The dead man poisoned himself and left no letters as to why he did what he did. Nothing.

The said man was found dead, by his cousin, and have committed self-murder one morning in the guest room at the latter's house. He had no trace of illness whatsoever. Yet his death only signified resistance to his bereaved family as what the rumors said.

"You were with him. How could you not stop him?" cried the best friend with her heart jumping out of her chest because of anger while gripping her hand from shaking involuntarily.

The cousin got offended and defended himself, saying, "He loved only you. Turning down his proposal made him feel broken all the more. And you dare to put the blame on me for not keeping eyes on him?"

Her tears left her eyes as she softly spoke the words, "If he and I did marry, the heavens would never rejoice. You know I loved someone else. And it's not my fault if you have loved your dear cousin more than anything or anyone in the world."

He was speechless at the notion and informed her instead, "Tomorrow is his burial. His family told me to deny your attendance."

"But they never allowed me in his wake. Aren't they too cruel for doing such?"

"I hope this is the last time we see each other, Mary," he uttered, trembling with all his insides regretting every word that came out from his lips. "I cannot be friends with you after this tragedy."

"If we can never be friends, then we can never be anything but foes, Eddie," she replied as she wore her hat. "And if we meet, may it be in hell, for I am certain to be seeing you there after what you have done today."

It was a gloomy day for them. They were breaking the bond they built because of a love that wasn't returned. And as they stood to leave the place, they never looked at each other. They just separated ways as if their meeting did not happen. Both the man and woman shared the burden of being the reason why the dead man killed himself. Yet it was the former who was talked of mostly for causing the terrible scandal.

Since that day, the woman, who was Maria Kristova, never wore other colors but black and was mourning forever. And the man, Edward Coldwell, remained a bachelor to atone for his mistakes as he believed he lost his heart and could never love again.

Madam Kristova woke up crying in the middle of the night. She still remembered that year her dear friend died, and vividly too, as if it was just yesterday. She did not kill him. She did not kill Tristan. Why would she? He was her closest whom she could never love as much as she loved the man who blamed her for his death.

Master Coldwell was not able to sleep that night as well. There were truths that he had no chance to tell Maria. Truths which would have ended the bad blood between their houses. Truths which would mark the beginning of their story together. Yet he seemed quite late for such and Maria's heart was filled with hatred towards him. If only he knew how to properly act in front of the woman he was fond of in the past, things would be absolutely different and better. But he did not and now he was tasting the bitterness of his own actions.

Chapter Eleven

It was church day and the Kristovas did go, but their gloomy party of four had taken everyone's attention. They were all dressed in black as if they were witches who were in town to collect ingredients like dark souls and wicked eyes to be kept in their jars. They found seats very close to the priest and to Maria Kristova's surprise, she seated beside her archenemy, Edward Coldwell, whom she often described in her mind as a fat toad. But he wasn't fat, nor a toad. He was actually looking different from all Maria's descriptions. Edward only greeted with a bow of the head, believing the woman beside him came to her senses. But Madam Maria, still feeling bitter towards him, did not do a thing.

The churchgoers were amused at the scene, but hopeful for the two houses to be on good terms again though everyone knew it was impossible. They were witnesses of how the two houses blamed each other about a Kovalski blood who committed self-murder many years ago. Yet the time was already due for the houses. However, everyone agreed that a miracle was needed and their prayer was for no more blood to be offered in the end. Though the root cause of such bickering was still unknown to them, they were sure there was more to the blaming. And only the master of

Coldwell Mansion, Madam Kristova, and the dead man from the Kovalski House knew everything.

Still, we must not forget the two young bloods who started answering everyone's prayers that day. Elric never failed to glance at Antonia and the lady did the same. Only their eyes did the talking that time and everybody was unaware of such a silent conversation. Even though the church was filled with singing and the warm sermon from the priest, both of the two only heard the beating of their own hearts as if there was a thunderstorm inside.

The sermon of the padre that Sunday was about loving the enemy as you have loved thyself. Edward Coldwell reckoned himself being on that road already, but the madam beside him did not consider that road at all. Loving him made her heart broken in the end and hateful and bitter. Though it's a mistake, a sin to hate, Maria Kristova would gladly do it over and over again.

The mass ended and it lifted the madam's heart from her chest. She felt as if an evil spirit was expelled from her body. But she was somewhat empty from the process.

Edward Coldwell, he stood outside the church waiting for Maria Kristova to come out. The man waited forever for this day, to make amends and ask for forgiveness. But he changed his mind as soon as the woman he expected passed him by like he was just a ghost she neither saw nor felt. "Witch!" he grumbled.

From the church, Madam Kristova's party proceeded to the marketplace. Maria and Juliet went inside a fabric store to buy silk and satin. Katarin and Antonia stayed outside the building and observed the busy people walking and working in one place and another.

Not too distant from them Katarin spotted familiar faces in an alley. The gentleman was giving the lady a pouch, and the latter seemed to be refusing. And Katarin was right, she knew them. The gentleman was Mr Kovalski, her uncle's friend, and the lady was the one she met at the tea shop, Miss Pierce. She became curious about their relationship. Were they lovers? Maybe. Maybe not.

Miss Pierce then hugged Mr Kovalski after accepting the pouch. Both parted ways when the encounter was over. While watching the scene, Katarin did not notice her twin sister left her side, who was hypnotized by a nearby bakery.

Antonia was full of bliss as she loved eating all sorts of food— heavy and light, sweet and sour, savory and everything. Her eyes were glittering as she entered the pastry house.

"Hello, miss!" The baker was smiling at her like she was an angel who'd grant all of his wishes.

"The smell is amazing!"

"Thank you! And what would you like to have?"

"Everything," Antonia gasped.

"That seems impossible," joined by another voice at the door which was very familiar to Antonia, whom she did not give any of her attention to because she was under the bakery's spell.

"But it is possible. I'll give her one of each kind," disagreed the baker.

"Thank you, Mr Baker," Antonia smiled at the baker before looking at the man who was confident to join someone else's conversation.

"I wasn't talking about the bread," the man uttered after his identity was revealed.

"And I wasn't talking to you either, Mr I-should-not-be-talking-to," teased Antonia when she realized it was Elric Coldwell.

"Really, now?"

"Aren't you supposed to be guarding your uncle?"

"He is with the spirits."

"What spirits?" she grinned. "Did you just kill him?"

"With spirits I mean the liquor boutique."

Antonia laughed. She did not catch his humor as soon as he dropped it. What a shame! She was supposed to be mentally alert. Maybe the pastry house did something great on her brains, considering she always loved studying intoxicating liquids. Never did she imagine the word spirit could be applied to alcohol as well. She was curious before about how it was possible to make people free their hidden beasts when they were drunk. Now she was sure it was because of the spirit. It could possess anyone at any time.

"What about you? Where is your family?"

"Outside, I guess. Haven't you seen them?"

"Only your sister. She looked like a statue outside."

"Really? Did she see you?"

"If her back has eyes, she might."

"How did you know I wasn't her?"

"I saw you getting in. You looked like a pup following the smell of food inside the bakery."

"A pup?"

"But a pup is cute."

"Am I cute?"

"If you're in a puddle."

Antonia teased, "You're evil."

"Well, I am not the one whose hair is red."

"I know," she smirked. "It is a belief that redheads are evil. Maybe I should change its color. What do you say?"

"Just let it be."

"And why is that?"

"So no one will get near you except for me."

"How vile! What's your point exactly?"

"I won't see you after today," he confirmed her thoughts. He almost said her name but stopped himself. "And I feel uneasy to think that you'll have new companions and will eventually forget me."

"We are not companions." Antonia's sadness was apparent when she accepted the paper bag from the baker and traded it with a small bag of coins.

"But you understand my point, do you not?"

She dragged Elric to a secluded corner while he was eyeing the street through a window. "Tell me what happened?"

"My uncle is sending me to the north garrison," he finally admitted.

"North garrison?" Antonia's eyes widened. "Did he find out?"

"Maybe a little, but not the entire thing. He told me about the news last week."

"Why are you only telling this now?"

"I did not want to spend time with you and have you worried about the day of my departure." Elric gave a heavy sigh as he confessed. "I wanted for you to have a good time with me. I needed to carry the burden alone of not seeing you for two years or maybe forever. Your eyes were too joyous to foresee a friend leaving at a certain time."

"I don't know what to feel," Antonia grumbled. "Must I be offended that you don't want to share such a burden with me? Or should I be happy that you value me so much you do not want me to worry?"

"Forgive me."

"There is nothing to forgive. I just hope this won't be the last time we see each other," she reached for his sleeve. "I wish I could trade places with you. Please, come back alive."

"Can I send you letters?"

"Of course." The woman felt hopeful. Elric's company became one of the best things that has happened to her in the capital. Not hearing from him again would be a great loss. Not seeing him again would be worse. "I'll wait," she added without looking at him, "for the letters. For you."

"Will you pray for me too?"

"You don't need to ask for something that will surely be done."

"Till we meet again." Elric took his leave without saying the woman's name nor hugging her tightly, though he desired it immensely and almost acted on it but stopped himself, because of the fear that their secret companionship might be known.

A forlorn Antonia joined Katarin outside and became another statue beside her sister until their great-aunt and their mother came back.

The next morning, at dawn, Kristova Mansion was a mess. The madam of the house demanded the maidservants to prepare the luggage of her granddaughters. She was sending them that instant to the training school.

"But, madam, why with the sudden plan?" asked the head maidservant.

"Madam Constantin changed the schedule. Men are being sent to the garrisons and ladies are requested to volunteer, too. I am afraid for my girls. They are not yet suited for volunteer work. Their only escape is the training school."

"Everything will be ready, madam. We will quickly heed your demands."

"Antonia! Antonia!" Juliet Kristova was knocking at Antonia's room. She was shouting which made her daughter wake up.

"I'm awake." The young lady got up. "I'm coming!"

"What's happening? Is the house burning?" she asked as she opened her door.

"Quickly now, girl! Prepare yourself." The mother scavenged her daughter's cabinet for proper clothes.

"Are we leaving?"

"Not we. You and your sister."

"Where are we going?"

"Training school."

"Now? Why?" Antonia was still sleepy.

"Yes, darling, now! And no more questions, please. Just move!"

Madam Kristova and her group were walking apace from their house towards the next block. They took off as soon as a public carriage arrived.

Outside the building of the training school for ladies, young women were standing in line and were saying their farewells to their mothers and guardians. Maria Kristova and Juliet kissed their girls, too, relieved they had no need to volunteer at any garrison in the country before leaving them there.

While waiting, the Kristova sisters heard the real reason why they needed to be at the training school that day. Antonia felt worried for her father, for Elric, and for the country. She felt worthless too for not being able to help, needing more people for the war meant it was just getting worse. Most of the girls were crying because it seemed like the end of the world. But Antonia and Katarin remained composed, unyielding to show their deepest concerns even though they began to despise the world and humanity.

As the sun was rising, a parade of men in military uniform passed the street where the training school was located. Everyone's attention present in the area was taken by the lines of men who were marching towards where the war was happening. Some ladies blushed whenever men looked at their direction and a few portrayed fears for them. Nobody knew if they'd ever come back safe and sound.

Katarin noticed a man in uniform looking at the two of them. Yet as he was marching past them she observed he was staring at Antonia. And Antonia too was doing the same as she was standing up. They were intimately looking at each other.

Elric was heartsick to see Antonia while leaving the capital. He never prayed for such a meeting which meant parting all the same. But seeing her looking strong for him motivated him. He needed all the strength he could collect.

Antonia wanted to hug him by the moment their eyes met. But the fence was steel and was too high to hurdle. And a public scandal would make everything worse. All she did was stare at him with the utmost care, hoping the man on the other side of the barrier felt her prayers and wishes for his safe return, all of their safe return. She was puzzled by her emotions, too. She felt concerned about her secret friend, but her worry was too much for just a fellow like him. Maybe there was more. And she feared to even admit that. She thought to be only thinking he was too young to die. He never owned his life yet or became an artist at the least.

"Who was that?" Katarin asked her twin.

"I cannot say," Antonia replied, casting her eyes to the ground. "Forgive me."

Someone said parting is a sweet sorrow. But parting would never be sweet. Being aware that the object of your inclination would never come back in one piece or alive would never be sweet at all nor bittersweet even. Then you would hold on to hope. That god existed and would grant prayers. And until you would meet the one you adore again, you could only wait.

Chapter Twelve

Elric Coldwell was fortunate enough to come from an elite class. That way his uncle made some arrangements regarding his military service in advance. He was not assigned to the battlefield and spent his first months guarding the garrison. But he was not free from witnessing the aftermath of war. People were dying, losing limbs, turning into lunatics and being forgotten by their families and lovers. Some never received a reply to their letters and a few had broken engagements. What terrified him most was a father burying his son's corpse, both were sent to battle.

And one day, after many months under sufferance and abstinence from the mundanities he grew up in, a carriage of volunteers was delivered. The group, mostly women, was from the capital. They would be assisting the doctors and nurses in the medical tents and houses. Some would be assigned in the lavatory, kitchen and the cremation process.

Elric did not hope to see Antonia. He knew she was safe from the face of war at the time being. Yet a familiar face reminded him of the lady he wished to hear from. It was Elisa Peirce. She arrived together with the first batch of volunteers. They had the chance to exchange words about the capital and their mutual friend, Richard Kovalski, before Elric begged her to help him concerning an important matter.

"If it's fine with you, I want to borrow your name and have you send a letter to Antonia," he asked. "I'm getting mad every second in this place, Miss Pierce. And I worry about her most. I hope she is well and does not think of me so much, whether my limbs are amputated or that I am already dead."

Elisa thought for a while. It was too risky for her. What would Antonia's great-aunt think if she discovered that her granddaughter was communicating with the capital's lady escort?

"Please, Miss Pierce! If she will receive a letter with my name on it, who knows what our houses will do with us? But your name will not give us away. Besides, Katarin knows you."

"Is it love?" Elisa turned to Elric and evaluated his eyes.

"I do not know. But this is the first time I care for someone like this. And when we parted, I felt something inside me was ripped. I do not feel whole anymore. There is a missing space inside me that I can never fill with anything except for Antonia's presence."

"That is all I want to hear." She smiled. "I'll help you. Where will I send it?"

"She is at the training school as we speak."

"I know that place. Write this evening, and I will send it tomorrow."

After his shift that night, Elric wrote to his dearest friend, despite the many doubts he had in order to begin the letter.

Antonia,

How are you? I have been longing for the library and our talks about life and everything. I realized here that life will only be given to us once and I must live it well by doing what I really longed to do. Because once I lost it I would never have it back nor experience all that I wanted.

The horrors of war are too much to bear. I have seen the worst and it is breaking my heart. I hope it will end soon. I am not sure if you will be happy to know that my childish nature is leaving me, too, because of everything that's happening here. I am more responsible now and I know what I want to do with my life. I saw the value of having a voice. One must say what he needed to say before he could not speak. One must listen before he could not hear. One must see what he wanted to see before he got blind. One must feel before he could become numb. And one must own his life before he could no longer author it. I hope to never become a ghost who'd keep haunting others for the lack of fulfillment in life.

And I pray this will reach you.

Always,

Elisa pierCe

For months Antonia Kristova tried adjusting to the training school with every ounce of difficulty. Staying in a room with nothing but a bed, a table, and a chair made her want to escape. Not die but escape. She never thought, even once, to commit self-murder. She believed she had a lot of things to do than to just end everything, nor to stay inside a room and be isolated from the world. Yes, there would be pain and suffering. But nothing would last forever, even heartaches. And with heartaches there would be learning. With learning there would be change. With change there would be growth.

One unexpected day Antonia was summoned to the headmistress' office. While heading there she checked every possible way to get out of the place.

"Antonia, a letter arrived from the garrison." Madam Diana Constantin, a stern-looking woman in her early forties, was on her table, acting like someone who owned everyone.

Antonia's eyes almost fell from their sockets upon knowing but did not say a word.

"I know we educate you about privacy and all, but I needed to check the content. I was warned about one of your hobbies— escaping."

The youngling remained silent, thus the older woman added, "The letter is from a woman."

Antonia was relieved to hear that the sender was a woman. Maybe Elric pretended as the other gender for that purpose, she had been waiting for a letter from him, and him alone. She knew nobody in town, only him. Besides it was solely Elric who promised to write to her.

"If it was from a man, you'd never receive it at all." Madam Constantin stood and handed Antonia the letter. "It's pure fiction, my dear, to know what our hearts want."

Antonia brought the letter to her room with an anguished heart, knowing the headmistress read the letter. When she read Elisa Pierce was the sender with odd capitalizations, she deduced it was from Elric Coldwell as she had expected. And she felt the sender's sorrow in every word as she absorbed the message, furthermore, moved by the realizations. She wished she could do more than offering him prayers and writing a reply, like fighting the outlanders alongside him or fixing bandages like nurses did. She never feared blood. She adored it.

dEarest Creature,

I received your letter and was devastated to imagine the atrocities of war you've witnessed for the duration of your service. And like you, I long for our times together as well, the freedom we attained in a secluded room and the ideas our minds exchanged. But we can never go back. We can only move forward. I wish I could do something more than writing this letter to ease the pain and distress you have. But you never failed to be in my prayers every night. Just like how I do pray for my papa.

I am happy about your new perspective in life. And I agree that a life once lived to its fullest is a hundred times of greater value than a thousand lives lived with missing pieces. And if someday you will be a ghost with a discontented heart, I want you to haunt me, for I once dreamt of seeing one and handing it my servitude. However, I would be more than happy to see you again, alive and breathing, and in one piece.

I am doing fine in the training school, though I have a hard time adapting. You know I never liked staying inside the house. You might be outside, but I know you're trapped, too. We are in different places but we are suffering just the same. Yet you will be proud of me once I get out of here, as well. I promise.

The next time we meet, let's reach our dreams together. I'll be with you through it. After all, I am your friend. God will bring you back to the capital, I know.

Write to me again.

Waiting,

Antonia

Elric's first year in the north garrison consisted of nights reading Antonia's replies to his letters and being moved by them; guarding his post for hours, thinking of what he would do once the war ended; stargazing at midnight till dawn and wishing for a better world; writing to Antonia again and missing her even; gossiping with Elisa and sharing Richard's secrets; longing for Antonia's red head and crazy mind; painting using anything he could find in the area; running here and there to ease his mind of chaos; and everything just to avoid insanity.

Antonia's first year in the training school was made of days in her room to contemplate on her mistakes but busied herself in altering her hair color after learning how to; in the dining hall with other girls to be educated how to eat quietly and to choose the right cutleries for certain dishes; in the drawing room with four other girls to practice how to accept and deny visitors; in the study to read books, which she liked, and to sit properly when doing so, which she despised; in the workshop to cultivate their interests like sewing, painting, lettering and sketching; in the kitchen to master cookery where she preferred eating everyone's edible results of their efforts, giving them ideas on their dishes, and washing the plates after burning her area; and in the backyard to be kissed by the sun which she liked despite the walk for hours to memorize the gait of a proper lady by wearing high-heeled shoes.

After a year, however, Madam Kristova discovered Antonia's dealings with Elisa Pierce. Madam Constantin talked to the former about the matter because the woman had an infamous name on her forehead due to her line of work. It was the cause why Antonia was allowed neither to write letters nor to receive one from anyone. Madam Kristova then decided to collect all Antonia's incoming letters after knowing that her granddaughter burned the ones she already received and studied.

Having no replies from Antonia, Elric believed she was exposed and he informed Elisa about it. That day she told her of the news another letter came. Elisa gave it immediately to Elric, but he returned it to her after opening it. Elric knew it was not written for him. Everything was different, the salutation, the handwriting, and the sender. It was from his friend, Richard Kovalski, sent especially for Elisa Pierce. Elric read nothing and uttered nothing. He understood their situation very well. Like Elric and Antonia, Richard and Elisa were also victims of society— their judgement, blood feud and dreadful ambitions.

Chapter Thirteen

When Elric was given his freedom week, a seven-day rest for those who completed a year of service in the military, he rode home to discuss his future plans with his uncle. He decided to tell him the truth about his love for painting. As he was traveling he prayed to the heavens for support and understanding from his dear uncle to be bestowed upon him.

Being banned from writing and receiving letters, Antonia considered herself caged. That was why she asked her twin sister for help. "I will be a lunatic if I won't get out of this asylum even for a day," she pleaded. "Please act on my behalf. Pretend that you are Antonia when they seek my presence. Please, Katarin, I beg of you."

Katarin knew Antonia. She would never stop planning just to get out nor asking for her help. And what could a day away from the training school do? It wouldn't possibly offer harm, would it? So, Katarin, for the love of her twin sister, helped her, but it was only for a day. Antonia escaped the training school wearing a servant's uniform. She slipped into the backyard, saw a gardener's hat and coat, and took them. Then she was free even though it was only for a day.

Since Antonia couldn't go home, she planned to march towards the library. She passed by the librarian stealthily and ran into the storeroom. Her vision was then graced by Elric's figure. She blinked not just once but five times to make sure it was him and his face did not vanish under the sun's light.

"E-E-Elric?" she stuttered out of surprise. "I-i-is that you?"

"It's—" Antonia hugged the man before he could finish his sentence.

She whispered, "You're alive. You're alive," in happiness.

That was the first time they ever hugged each other. Both were thankful for the moment they were in the same room. Both hopeful to see their faces each day without end if it was even possible.

"And you're Antonio," Elric commented. "Why did you escape training school?"

"They forbid me to accept, to write, and to send letters. And you know I cannot handle a day being inside the house when forced."

"That's why I never received a reply," he realized as she left his embrace, smiling. "But I am glad you are well. Where did my letters go then?"

"To my great-aunt, of course. I hope she won't discover us. I burned the ones I opened, making her suspicious. How many letters did you send?"

"A lot."

"Did you write something odd?"

"Perhaps." Elric could remember writing a subtle confession. "And what happened to your hair? Haven't I told you not to change it?"

"Oh, this," she pulled a strand and laughed. "I learned how to alter its color. They taught us to. And it is helpful. Katarin and I look exactly the same. They won't know I am gone."

"Pretty clever."

Antonia teased, "But how did you know it's Antonia, and not Katarin?"

"Katarin does not defy the rules nor wear a man's clothing," he returned.

"You are right. What about Miss Pierce? How did it happen that you used her name?"

"She was stationed in my garrison. She's a volunteer. Forced to volunteer, I'd say. But she was indeed a blessing. Her presence lessened my loneliness and my longing for life in the capital. And she helped me write to you."

"Are you done with your service?" Antonia went to a corner with a new arrival of books. "Are you free? Because I only have today. I must be back in the training school before tomorrow comes."

"I am out for a week," Elric tailed her, "it's my third day today. I have been in the library mostly since I arrived, remembering you. And I spoke with my uncle, too, regarding being an artist."

"Did he accept?" she faced him, his eyes gleaming.

"No," he shared, without hiding his dismay. "He wants me to crack my head open for another year. Think things over." He could still recall how his uncle hollered angrily at his admission.

"I am sorry to hear such news, Elric." She thought of her plan, "I think—" and doubted if she should tell him about it.

"Think what?"

"I. Well—"

"Spill the beans, Antonia." He shook her, his arms on her shoulders.

"I think there is a solution to our problems."

"What is it?"

"It's outside," she informed Elric as she dragged him to the newspaper stand outside the library. "This!" pointed Antonia at an announcement.

"An expedition to the east?"

She nodded in reply.

"I don't understand."

"Keep reading." And Elric did, silently, as Antonia spoke, "This huge ship needs painters and writers for the journey. You and I are just what they want."

"Are you sure about this, Miss Kristova?" he jested. "You are neither a painter nor a writer, but a heavy drinker."

Antonia laughed but was holding her voice down. "I write, Mr Coldwell, believe me. I study wine and I write about it too. I also wrote stories, you know. And I thought about this for a million times already."

"You just knew this today since you escaped training school. How can you think about it for a million times?"

"I think while I think. I told myself every second the moment I read this a while ago to go. I don't talk numbers but I am certain to have told myself to go. For a million times."

"Your math is not mathing, my lady. And that's not thinking, that's telling yourself."

"They are just the same, kind sir. But we have no time to debate on that. So, are you in?"

"This means it's confidential, is it not?"

Antonia nodded. "Of course."

"When will this ship dock in the capital's port?"

"Within another year, or two."

"Can you wait that long, Miss Kristova? It will be difficult for you."

"Well, yes!" She was quite eager. "One can wait for something that's sure to come."

"What if it will not?"

"Stop being so negative, Mr Coldwell," she whispered. "It will ruin your mind."

Elric touched his arms to hers. "What do we need to be accepted for employment then?"

"By sending our works, of course!" She pointed at an address. "There."

He realized it was quite near. "We can get there on foot. Do you already have your piece to send?"

"I will write it on the way." She raised a brow at him. "I am thinking of a poem."

"You're really amazing, are you not?" His smile was as bright as the midnight sun. "All right, come with me to my uncle's place. I need a diversion to get one painting."

"Can you not make one on the way?" Antonia complained.

"It won't dry in time. Let's go."

"But a sketch using a pen can do."

He started pacing towards home. "I am not motivated to draw something that will suffice right now. Stress is stressing me out."

She followed, grumbling, "Fine. Let us have fun walking together."

Antonia was astonished to see the Coldwell Mansion. It was all white and totally opposing the dark facade of Kristova Mansion on the other side of the capital. However, it appeared much colder than the latter. Madam Kristova's house might be dark but there was warmness in its physical aspect, homelike to be specific.

Elric and she tried their best not to get attention upon entering the huge building, but Edward Coldwell himself noticed them in the hallway as they walked past him. He was standing on a terrace.

"Elric, where have you been?" He was hopeful his nephew was not upset anymore about their talk on painting the other day. But he was surprised by the funny figure tailing Elric. "And who is this little man you're with?"

"Antonio," the nephew quickly replied. "Of the Noirs. He is a fellow from the garrison."

Edward was suspicious. "I haven't heard of such a name from that house."

"He is not from the capital," Elric added as if he was saying the truth.

"Well, then. Enjoy your visit, Mr Noir," was what Sir Coldwell uttered before he left them.

Antonia only bowed her head as a reply. Talking would jeopardize everything.

Inside his room Elric opened a trunk full of his sketches and paintings in small canvases. He scanned for the perfect piece without noticing Antonia stealing a woman's portrait.

"Why did you do this?" Antonia asked by showing him his painting of her. It was not debatable, the artwork certainly looked like her.

Elric, feeling embarrassed, tried grabbing the portrait but the young lady swiftly evaded him.

"Elric?" she teased. "Why?"

"You know why."

"Tell me. Please."

"This is so embarrassing," he mumbled as he palmed his forehead.

"Since when did you feel embarrassed towards me?"

"Stop it or—" Elric moved closer to Antonia, almost kissing her. He wished for her to feel he had confirmed his affection for her.

"Or what?" Antonia asked again, but in proud defiance, her hand holding the portrait was above them. It made Elric stop himself.

"I want that," he whispered in her ear. Yes, he wanted that portrait, for employment. And he wanted her, for him.

Antonia, to her shock, slammed his artwork on his chest without uttering a word. She was thinking he fancied her for him to do the sketch. And she felt a huge disappointment towards herself because of the assumption. She was in distress regarding the closeness they just had, too. It was as if she was playing with fire which could turn her into ashes in just a matter of seconds. She hated the feeling from thinking that he would kiss her. It suffocated her.

"What was the violence for?" was all Elric said, feeling mischievous about what he did.

"Don't mess with me, Coldwell," she warned him as she went for the doors.

He scrambled to his feet and stopped Antonia from leaving by hugging her. And tightly he did despite it was her back that was facing him. Yet he never imagined, even a bit, that he would become the main object of everyone's gossip in the capital because of such an act.

Antonia's voice was soft, her chest stilled. "What are you doing?"

"I miss you."

She almost cried though felt relieved. "But I am still here." She realized the touch of his warmth which permeated from the fabric of her suit to her pale skin made her feel safe. And she wanted all of it for her.

"But it feels like a dream."

Antonia then gingerly removed Elric's hand from her, the other still holding the portrait, and she kissed the product of their first meeting, the scar on his palm. "This is true. We are real."

A maidservant passed by the room's window, witnessed the intimate situation and thought Edward Coldwell's heir was into men. She shared the details to another servant who also mentioned the confidential information to a gardener.

Four days later, just when he went back to the garrison, the name Elric Coldwell, next master of Coldwell Mansion, was labeled as a man who preferred men over women, confirming the theories which for years circulated as to why he never had explicit affairs like his fellows. And it was a scandal that the capital was feasting over for weeks, then months, as if every soul were hungry vultures.

Chapter Fourteen

Richard Kovalski decorated the office of Mr Qalif, a talkative and inquisitive man who was useful in his kind of business. Mr Qalif, a marketeer, was the employer for Expedition VII. His place was located at the docks.

Richard was there on a friend's behalf who badly needed employment on the ship. "I can recommend a person who can entertain the people boarding the ship."

"Aren't you too early, Mr Kovalski?" The old man lit his cigar after pouring himself a glass of whiskey.

"Didn't they say the early bird gets the worm?"

Mr Qalif offered Richard another glass but he refused. "Tell me about this person. Is he good? Will my money be given justification?"

"I assure you, she will."

"We are talking about a woman, I see. Is she the infamous lady escort?"

"I do not agree she is infamous." Richard gripped the hat he was holding. "And she has a name. It is Elisa Pierce."

"But her identity will ruin my image. I can't let that happen, Mr Kovalski." Mr Qalif adjusted his seat as he asked Richard to take his.

"Mr Qalif, please." The man before him was akin to a wretched one upon sitting on a bench inside the marketeer's office. Anxiety was apparent on his face. "She is not what you think she is. She is not selling her body the way people imagine. She is entertaining people, not seducing men. She makes people laugh and happy with all her stories and jokes. And she is very good at it."

"You seem to like her."

"Well, what is not to like about her?" He huffed. "But I am here to help her and not to confess anything as if I committed a crime or something."

"I am not playing detective to have you confess things. I am no judge either, but I'm listening."

"She's in the garrison right now." Richard's eyes wandered the walls in the room. Old photos of ships were hung there together with some peculiar trinkets and outlandish antiques. "After a year she'll be done volunteering. And she will need to be employed somewhere she is good at. And she's good at humoring people. I bet my name on it."

"I will give you the benefit of the doubt." Mr Qalif stood to look outside the window. The sky was getting dark. "You just have her employed."

"Thank you, Mr Qalif. You will never regret it."

Richard Kovalski wore his hat to leave the office, but before he could the old man asked him about another matter. "Do you happen to know anything about the Coldwell Mansion?"

"Yes, I have a close fellow from that house."

"And have you heard about the rumor?"

"What rumor?"

The marketeer turned to Richard. "The heir of that house prefers men than women."

"Elric?" The question was answered positively, thus he inquired again to clarify the claim. "Do you mean Elric Coldwell, the heir to Sir Edward, is into men?"

Mr Qalif nodded. "It's been out there for weeks."

"What in seven hells?! I don't agree!"

"Are you certain he is not?"

"I am. And I will bet my name on it, too." Richard looked weary now. The rumor was absurd and could ruin House Coldwell. "He is in the garrison at this very moment. Why do you ask about him?"

"He handed in a portrait." Mr Qalif went back to his table and pulled a drawer. "You see, the expedition needed people who would write down everything during the voyage."

"And he wanted to be employed as well?"

"Not just him but a woman, too. They were here together which surprised me, because the woman's name was Antonia Kristova."

"Are you sure?"

"Yes, and they were both good." The old man dropped two papers on his table, one was a portrait and the other a poem. "The man can draw and the woman can write."

Richard validated that the sketch was indeed done by Elric's hand. "That piece of art is undeniably his work."

"What do you think, Mr Kovalski? Should I accept them?"

"Why do I have to decide on such a matter?"

"We both know their houses are troubled."

"Those houses hate each other," Richard agreed at the thought. "But all I can say is if they are that good, they deserve the chance."

"What about you, Mr Kovalski? Are you not interested in joining your fellows?"

"I do not have the talent."

The concept made the marketeer laugh his heart out. "No one is of no talent, young man. You have at least a year to think things over."

"I don't know, Mr Qalif." Richard wore his hat again and said, "Maybe I will," before leaving the place.

That same day Maria Kristova visited her granddaughters in the training school and was fixed at one goal— scolding Antonia. She discovered her escape through Madam Constantin and feared for the young lady's stead. Her escapades would be of no advantage to her fate and could lead to her ruin or worse, her demise.

Inside Madam Constantin's office, Madam Kristova met the twin sisters. "Katarin, you have something to tell me, have you not?"

The young lady lied and said no before adding, "I have nothing to tell, Aunt Maria."

"Liar!" Madam Kristova bellowed.

The accusation was gladly accepted but Katarin did not show weakness. Antonia, beside her, felt absolutely guilty and interfered. "It was all mine, Aunt Maria. She did nothing."

"Where did you go that day?"

"Library." It was true but it wasn't the only place she had gone to. "The library."

"The next time you do this I will throw you out of my house!" Madam Kristova warned in a thunderous voice. "And if you, Katarin, will help her, you will suffer the same!"

"Yes, Aunt Maria," the twin siblings chorused.

"You can leave now," Madam Kristova said firmly, "Katarin."

Katarin glanced at Antonia before leaving Madam Constantin's office. Both looked exactly the same now. If Antonia did not change her hair color they'd be easy to spot. But their secret of that day wouldn't be discovered if only Madam Constantin did not request for both of their presence in her office. The madam's sleuthing skill was something to loathe because she could always find out even the tiniest acts of felony done by the ladies she had been training.

"I am glad Madam Constantin told me about your escape. Do you really think you can fool me? Even if you change the color of your hair, your eyes are still faded brown!" Madam Kristova's rage reverberated in the room. "Katarin has darker ones!"

"Forgive me, Aunt Maria. I am not trying to defy you at all. Neither to escape completely."

"Then why did you escape in the first place? You did that once, you can do it again. What are you planning?"

Antonia stuttered a few answers. "I. I. I just wanted to breathe. E-E-Even for a day. I-I promise you, it won't happen again."

"And what about Elisa Pierce? I read the letters she addressed to you. Her words seemed like she's in love. With you."

"What do you mean?"

"Do you like her?"

"I like Miss Pierce. She is a good person."

Madam Kristova's eyes widened in surprise. "Is there more?"

"What can be more? Miss Pierce and I are merely acquaintances. Katarin and she, they knew each other."

"Good," the older woman exhaled a great deal as if something evil left her body as soon as she heard Antonia's answer. "Elisa Pierce is family and she is you father's first cousin," she confessed before she marched out of the office without waiting for Antonia's reaction.

Antonia exited after a minute, still baffled about Elisa Pierce being a relative, yet relieved for not being completely caught by her great-aunt.

Chapter Fifteen

Wilfred West joined Richard Kovalski's walk at the park one afternoon. Information came to him about Expedition VII and the fact that an Arab princess sponsored the said journey.

"I know about that expedition, it is a trip to the east. But I was not aware of its sponsor," was Richard's reply to his information.

"Are you not interested, Rich? I bet wealthy people will be on that ship."

"Wil, we cannot leave the capital that easily."

"Who said about leaving? 'Tis traveling! We will be back in no time."

"I have been thinking about it though." Richard always wanted to escape his parents, their claws and the capital's prying eyes.

"Tell me when you have decided. I will start from there."

Richard scratched his temple. "Why do you have to know my plans?"

"Because we are friends. I do not want to be on that ship alone. You know I am not brave enough. I am the coward amongst us."

"Then I will inform you the moment I will come up with a final decision."

"Great!"

A gust of wind interrupted their walk which made them realize the early arrival of winter. But to Richard, it reminded him of the rumor that had been circulating around the capital for weeks. "Wilfred, haven't you heard?"

"Heard of what?"

"A rumor."

"What rumor?"

"Of course, you did not. It is pure madness actually. And I don't believe it either."

"What is it?"

Richard shook his head caused by disbelief. "Women are laughing, and men are mocking our Elric."

"But why? What did he do?"

"They say he is into men."

"That's ridiculous! Of course, it is not true. We know him very well to disagree on that issue."

"Someone saw him being intimate with a man in his room."

"Really?"

"That is what I heard."

"How intimate?"

"Hugging. And kissing."

"What?! But is he not in the garrison?"

Richard had a positive response and added that Elric was back for a week sometime last month.

"Was he?"

"Do not use it against yourself. He did not show himself to me either."

"I hope he is well. I hate the garrisons."

"We all hate the garrisons."

"Yet if he is," Wilfred continued the discussion on Elric's preference, "as what they have said, there is nothing wrong with it, I think. Won't you agree?"

Richard puffed, "There is absolutely nothing wrong, but society will not allow it."

"But society won't matter," the other insisted. "As long as you are happy and not hurting others, it is fine by me."

"Still, it is offensive to the church and to religious institutions."

"If it is, then why do they treat homosexuals lesser than those who had extramarital affairs, Rich? As if it's a greater sin than the other."

"It is a complete tragedy."

"God, save humanity."

After Elric's rumor spread in the capital, Antonia's inclination to a woman followed. Both houses became objects of derision, and that distressed the master and madam of each house. They were once again, after many years, the center of attention in the capital.

The idea of loving the same gender was considered a human abnormality at the time. It was scandalous and obscene, something worthy to be publicly condemned. In accordance with religious institutions, men were created for women, and women for men. People who did not conform to this were labeled immoral.

Edward Coldwell sent an urgent letter to the north garrison, requesting the captain to deliver his nephew to the south. He did so out of fear the rumor might crawl its way to where his nephew was and that it would humiliate him. He also wrote a letter to the Noir clan in Primus, concerning the veracity of an Antoine Noir's identity, who was the only man that had appeared in the mansion when Elric was home again for a short time. The letter received a reply two weeks later, verifying that there was no Antoine Noir in their registry of births. Edward was enraged and suspicious of his nephew. Elric was becoming more and more unpredictable, and impossible to control.

Maria Kristova did something too. She bribed whisperers about Antonia's issue and revealed that both ladies were her kin, that Elisa Pierce used to live in Kristova Mansion a few years back, and that the madam accepted and supported her interest in the entertainment industry. She also told the talebearers that even if Antonia did love a woman, she'd never throw her out of her house. Anyone could always love anybody. Why must they be judged when everyone did the same though in different ways? The madam quite had the vigor to repel every rumor by embracing all the oddities that the public had ever thrown at her house. From being named a witch by generating products which prolonged beauty to being called a Lilith, a she-devil, by having a deranged family line, Maria proudly and gracefully drank and devoured them all.

The scandal became immense that it crept unto the royal throne. Though the king and queen remained silent about the rumor, realizations were brought up regarding the love for the same gender. Everyone needed the love they could find in all four directions of the country. It was not wrong as long as nobody was harmed, except for tradition and old belief which should be already buried six feet below the ground.

Debates happened between men, while women remained soft on the issue. What should be classified as immoral and evil was the existence of paramours, the copulation outside marriage, the abuse against spouses and partners, the irresponsibility of a parent, and so much more to mention.

However, there were women, like Isabel West, who believed it was being ungrateful of both genders to prefer the union between their own genders. War was at hand, people were dying. Women were ought to have more births and replace the loss of men. Though her concept was not wrong, it was not as well right.

Consent must be given before a situation, later was the accountability of both parties. Both must first agree to wed, and both must be responsible for the consequence, their union and their children. Both must be involved, because both started it to begin with. But if one side failed to be accountable and strong, the other should not be expected to remain standing for the rest of the season.

Yet humanity would lie somewhere in the foot of these unions. It might require two individuals to create a family, the smallest unit of society, but it would take a village to raise a child. And if this child could not feel love in between, it would either burn the village to the ground just to feel its warmth or pacify itself to lift the burden from the land. Either way, the children were always the collateral damage. Either way, it would take strong souls to act upon. These children, these helpless ghosts which would become the public and the rulers of the future, all wrecked and done. Who should take the blame? Who should carry the shame? Should we all not embrace them when we were all nothing but the same?

The elephant of a scandal, like all other scandals, withered in time. The public quieted, got bored at the debates, and the rumors eventually subsided. Months passed and the gossip pertaining to the two houses were considered shelved.

Chapter Sixteen

Within a year, the scandal about the houses Kristova and Coldwell was replaced by another huge and dreamy subject. It was literally huge and dreamy because it was a ship, said to be clad in steel that the entire population of noblemen in the country could fit. And it was on its way towards Simetra.

Ship Maharlika's interior was expected to comprise eight hundred compartments for a group of four that only the elite class could afford. The other two hundred cabins with five beds were destined for those who would be employed on the ship.

Expedition VII reached all doors and every Ashmetrean was astonished. Problems were given a halt, each one wanted to be on that enormous boat. And it was indeed the most opportune time to leave the country if one was not willing enough to see the remnants of war in the north and south regions.

At the south garrison men and women were rejoicing because the war finally ceased that year. They gained victory with the enemy's retreat. Everyone in the service celebrated, though saddened still by the loss of countless men. Soldiers and volunteers started to head home except for Elric. Before he took the road towards the capital he offered the commanding officer of his troop the help of restoring his home out of gratitude for the goodness and guidance that the older soldier bestowed upon him while he was in the south.

It took Elric a month to stay in the south. And he loved every day of it. He wrote to his uncle about it and was understood by him. Sir Coldwell even praised him for such an altruistic act. There, in the Land of the Unmarried Ones, Elric realized it was a good thing to be alive. He learned to love nature, soil and hard work. He got to learn carpentry, too, and comprehended how fulfilling it was to restore a house with your bare hands, blood and sweat.

Sir Kallistar, as he was called that way in the garrison, lived in a small town in the south. It was rich in red soil and rivers. He owned the land, his birthright, where he built his home and never left it since. His closest neighbor would take an hour of walking. They rode horses most of the time, because public carriages passed only once a week, and on a Sunday.

He was a kind man, Elric observed, and a good father. Sir Kallistar did not mention his children often but when he did he was quite admirable. He was the silent type, and only talked when needed or when he had something great to say about the trees and life.

"What are your plans, Erradyn, after the war?" he asked one afternoon while they were doing some wood work. Erradyn was Elric's pseudonym in the military.

"I told someone to meet her at the docks."

"Are you going to elope?"

"We are going to live the lives we wanted," Elric shared. "We are not eloping. How I wish she loved me the way I love her."

"You did not say anything?"

"I wanted to but I hesitated."

Sir Kallistar inquired why and Elric replied with a forced smile. "I thought I would not live to see the end of war. I thought I would die in battle. I did not desire for her to break and be wretched because of me."

"Did you not know? Grief is said to be the price we pay for love."

"But what if she does not love me the way I do?"

"It is also said that 'tis better to love and fail than not trying to love at all."

Elric shook his head. "I do not know. I just feel so afraid."

"But which is of greater weight, your fear of the unknown or your love for her?"

"Good question. It's the answer."

"You are welcome."

"Well, how did you meet your wife?"

It was Sir Kallistar who forced a smile this time. He said that he saw her at a ball for the first time and fell for her the moment their eyes met. She did not bow her head at him when he introduced who he was, she nodded. She nodded as if she agreed with him on something. And when he smiled, she gave him her hand and took him to the dance floor. By midnight he proposed to be her husband and she responded positively.

"What did you say?"

"I said I will love her every day."

"That easily?"

The older man smirked. "Her family was against it because she was already betrothed. My aunt did not like the idea either."

"You eloped?"

"We met again at the next ball and by dawn the following day we rode the public carriage towards Mayari, my hometown. We were blessed with two darlings later."

Elric was amazed by the tale. It was something you would only read in books. "Again, I am not eloping with this lady. She opposes the rules set by society for women. She hates being boxed. And I understand her more than anyone because I despised being controlled either by duty or by somebody."

"But that does not mean you cannot love her, Erradyn," he insisted. "Love her while you can. Love her before she is gone."

As a reply, Elric accidently hammered a finger. It bled and instead of being scared at it, like he was used to, he sipped the blood. It magically tasted like the sea instead of rust.

That same year, the twin sisters' training school days concluded. They graduated at last, and Antonia felt proud of herself. She just discovered she had another identity, someone who was a proper lady, for she believed she could never let go of her true self, the wildling.

Katarin and Juliet were happier because the former's twin sister behaved very well during the last year in the training school. Antonia had been following the rules she never liked. It was a bit odd because it was quite unlike her to follow what others expected of her.

But Madam Kristova was the happiest. The war ended and her twin granddaughters were safe. Also, they graduated from the training school with satisfactory outcomes.

Madam Constantin portrayed pride as well, she got to have a Kristova sit still. But her glory was short-lived because when she invited the Kristovas to her house one time, Antonia broke an expensive vase and did not say sorry.

"The vase was in the way," the naughty one claimed. "It should have not been there in the first place." Antonia even jested, "This house needs a new interior decorator." She spited Madam Constantin, the one who decorated her father's house.

Katarin elbowed her sister. "Your audacity to say whatever you want is killing me."

The other replied, "Did you not know your Aunt Isabel and the madam of this house used to bully my Aunt Maria and Madam Crossman?"

"Where did you get such detail about them?"

"I have my ways," winked Antonia.

"Did you just disown Aunt Isabel?" Katarin did not miss the detail in her twin sister's words a second ago.

"If she remains insensitive to other people's feelings, I will call her your aunt forever, not mine."

"I do not know why she has difficulty wearing someone else's shoes. Perhaps she is at war with herself too."

"I hope the good side of your aunt wins."

When the volunteers and soldiers from the garrison arrived home after the war, Antonia secretly met with Elisa to gather information on Elric. Though she said he was alive she had no idea where he had gone. Still, it made Antonia glad that the man she cared for remained in the mortal realm.

By the next few months Juliet decided to head home first when Rudolf, her husband, sent her a missive, bearing the good news that everything in town was back to normal. She said her farewells to her twin daughters and wished them to be embodiments of propriety. Antonia only grinned at it.

It was the season of the Great Nine, and since the war ended, most people were in the capital to meet connections and prospects. Katarin and Antonia then busied themselves with balls and dresses with their great-aunt, Maria, and her friend, Lili Crossman.

But Antonia was Antonia, she dreaded the dancing and seeking of husbands. What left her vigorous was her frequent visits in the monastery where the orphans were temporarily situated. She read them stories and children's books. Katarin, on the other hand, was tailing Isabel West to learn about managing balls.

The Queen's Ball that year had its theme on Roman myth. Despite the thunder and lightning outside the queen's palace, locals and outlanders filled the hall. The ladies to be introduced to the public that night wore white gowns, portraying as naiads. Katarin joined the ball with Isabel West.

Antonia was left at home, still deciding whether to join or not when Maria and Lili were drinking wine to their hearts' content. Yet something inside her was insisting to be at the Queen's Ball that night than completely drowning herself with the thoughts of Elric being dead when news of him in the capital had not yet reached her ears. Thus, she left her sleeping aunt and her aunt's friend by midnight, wearing the attire of Proserpina, Goddess of the Underworld.

Elric Coldwell was leaning at a column, his brunet locks on his shoulder, with a red wine in hand when a woman in black passed. Her scent was familiar but he stopped himself from minding her because he was yearning for Antonia. And his propensity to tell her the truth of his heart was suffocating him. Yet he could not stop himself from planning the days after the expedition, where to go next and what to do. However, his eyes could not resist to take a glimpse at the dance floor and that woman in black. He could only see her back. And her neck. And that red hair he had engraved in his memory after nights of her haunting him in his dreams. He left the column and put his wine glass in someone else hand to get a closer look of that woman on the opposite side of the ballroom.

When a music piece began, Antonia was revealed to own the face of that woman in black. She, in return, had to squint her eyes to make certain she was looking at Elric. She nodded at him when she noticed it was only his hair that had changed. They met in the middle of the room, and when he asked for her hand, she gave it.

"You are Pluto, from the underworld. Handsome. Mischievous. Yet Loyal," she told him as they began dancing.

He answered, "And you are Proserpina, forced to be in the underworld. Divine. Brave. And Untamable."

Both hearts were at bliss to see each other being safe and sound. And since their guardians were not there to keep watch, Antonia and Elric had that moment to themselves. Nobody cared about rumors and scandals. The war just ended and everybody deserved to let loose and free themselves from the reins made by duty or propriety.

"I adore your hair," he said a bit loudly for her to hear.

She beamed and teased him. "Everybody is afraid to get near me. They think I am a witch. So, pardon me for obliging you to a dance."

Elric was most pleased to have her for himself. "My uncle warned me again about my hair. He said I look like a girl," he shared.

"Don't cut it," Antonia countered. "Girls will be following you around if you do so. And I want you all for myself."

He, with long locks, brightened at the thought of her being jealous. "I miss you."

"I am here."

For the first time in a long time, Elric touched Antonia again. And she was still burning like a hearth, like home. His longing was then satisfied by her sincere smiles and intense stares. He thought that perhaps she loved him too.

Katarin saw her twin sister dancing with a man. It made her delighted. Antonia appeared to be enjoying every second of it. It was the first time that she saw her twin aglow, as for balls. "That is the young blood from Coldwell Mansion," murmured Isabel West on her side. "Too bad such happiness will not last forever. Efforts will be negated because those two houses despise each other, do they not?"

The ball ended at the first hour of dawn and when the attendees were leaving the hall, Antonia and Elric ought to say good bye. But the man could not seem to let go of the woman. He kept holding her tiny finger, which he had been doing for the remainder of the night. And she did not complain, she actually admired it. He was being possessive in the subtlest way in a sea of people.

"Elric," Antonia whispered as she held his hand, looking at the fading scar on his palm caused by their first encounter, "I am happy you are here."

He suppressed his tears as he saw her planting a kiss on the scar. "I am happy this is real," he returned because being with her always felt like a sweet dream and never true. Elric was unable to contain his gladness to be with Antonia that he hugged her tight, and tightly so. The scene was just enough to be misinterpreted they were betrothed.

"What is wrong?" she whispered.

"I never thought of ever seeing you again."

Antonia sighed. "Why?"

Elric wished to have the courage to tell her that he loved her immensely it was killing him in a way. The idea of their guardians being against them posed another threat. "Are you betrothed?" His question earned a hearty laugh from Antonia.

"That worries you?"

"I mean," he stuttered, "we cannot go on with the plan if you are."

Antonia grinned, "Even if Aunt Maria found me a man to marry, I am too stubborn to follow orders. You know that, do you not?"

"Forgive me," Elric forced a smile as he let her go. "I did not mean to doubt you. I just wanted to know. I heard your house will resume to look for prospects. As well as mine."

"Let us just pray that the ship will arrive in time. I do not wish to do the worst option either."

"What option is the worst?"

"Elopement."

Elric took a deep breath. "That is scandalous, indeed." Yet he was the most relieved of her reply.

"We both know that friendship between a man and a woman is against the norm. It is either they love each other so much they cannot be separated, or they hate each other they cannot be near one another."

"Like my uncle and your aunt?"

"Exactly."

"Tragic."

"So, should we say good night now?"

Elric could not stop himself and hugged Antonia again before parting with her and imagining she said, "I love you too."

Chapter Seventeen

The plan was still a plan even though Elric Coldwell and Antonia Kristova did not meet in secret nor accidentally, again, when everything went back to where it was before. They did not even try to, not to mention their houses kept avoiding each other which was why the two young spirits never had the chance for another encounter. Both waited and waited for Ship Maharlika. And between their waiting and doing other things, they were told about their scandals that the capital laughed at and feasted upon for weeks.

Elric's friends told him when they gathered together at a gentleman's liquor house called Oinos.

"It bothered me, really," mumbled Richard. "Until I saw you dancing with a woman in black at the Queen's Ball recently."

"You both attended?" Wilfred appeared exhausted.

"Did your parents not require it of you do so?" Elric raised his brows.

"It is a form of resistance."

"My mother forced me," added the other. "I obliged to avoid my father's bitter tongue."

Wilfred remembered to ask again. "So, who was the fortunate woman?"

Elric reddened at the thought that it was Antonia, Wildfred's niece. Richard saved him by saying, "The vision was blurry. I was standing from a distance and she was wearing a black veil."

"Elric?"

"Wilfred, I cannot tell anyone yet. My uncle has ears everywhere." He did not lie though. It was the truth. His Uncle Edward hated House Kristova for years, he would hate him too for loving and desiring one.

"I wish the woman was one of my nieces."

Richard smirked. "And have the two houses begin another war, considering the first has not yet ended."

"But tell us, who was that man you were with that day?" Wilfred investigated. He was slouching on his seat, his whiskey untouched.

"Did you really kiss him?" Richard seconded. "And why did you not visit us after your first year in the garrison?"

"Must you know?" Elric grumbled, earning him a loud "Yes!" from the two. "It was a woman, of course, dressed as a man. She was the woman in black. We were arguing about a portrait."

"You brought a woman to Coldwell Mansion?! In front of Sir Edward?! Dressed as a man?!" Wilfred laughed as if he was the happiest man alive. "And the old man believed the disguise?!"

"Only that time, I guess."

"Where did your audacity spring from?"

"From her," he smiled. "She is one wildflower, you see."

Wilfred stood and drank his whiskey to offer cheers, perhaps condolences, to his friend who was in a haze. "I adore romance and what it can do to a man! Even to the most dutiful one."

Richard went silent. He realized by then that the woman in black was Antonia, answering Wilfred's wish for the mysterious lady to be one of his nieces. He eyed Elric and beamed at him, teasing. When Wilfred left to get another shot of whiskey, it was Elric's turn to tease him.

"And you do not think Elisa Pierce and I did not meet in the garrison?"

Richard's bright smile vanished. He clinked his glass to Elric's and softly said, "Condolences to us, my dear friend! Condolences!"

Antonia was at the Black Market when Katarin told her about the scandal. They were heartily amused by it.

"What were you writing about? I heard they were love letters."

"It was merely a misinterpretation," Antonia giggled. She was palming a fabric at a stall.

"Really now?"

"And do you know? She is Kristova."

Katarin gasped. "Miss Elisa Pierce? No wonder she seemed to know much about Aunt Maria. She is family after all."

"She is a love child," whispered Antonia this time and earned another gasp from her twin.

"I like her. She is lovely and kind."

"I like her too."

After buying the fabric, both headed for home. But Katarin could not stop herself from thinking about the man Antonia danced with at the Queen's Ball.

"Why did you not tell me?"

Antonia paused. "About what?"

"About the young Coldwell."

"What do you mean?"

"You do not have to lie, Ant." Katarin held her twin sister's arm. "He was the man who went for the service that day we were sent to training school."

Antonia remained silent. She was found out by her twin. It would not be long before their aunt would know as well. Tears were forming in her eyes.

"I worry because it was Aunt Isabel who told me it was a young Coldwell you danced with that night."

"This is too much. Everything is just too much."

Katarin hugged her twin and cried with her. "What do you want to do?"

"I don't know, Kat." She sobbed. "I don't know anymore."

"Do you love him?"

Antonia bawled, like a child who lost a close friend, and it was unlike her. She never cried on matters big or small. Perhaps she was carrying a much greater burden this time.

"I love you, Antonia. I am here. And I will understand whatever it is you are trying to conquer within. I love you."

To make matters worse, Wilfred's carriage passed them and he insisted for his nieces to ride with him and his party of three. Thus, they all found themselves in a situation they did not prepare for.

Antonia's eyes were swelling and kept them casted on her lap. Elric was certainly worried about her and asked if she was fine. Katarin replied to the question on her sister's behalf, sharing that a huge bug had caused it. Richard was reading between the lines and jested Elric to stop bugging Antonia with queries because she seemed unwell. Wilfred, not knowing what was happening, suggested for them five to spend time together that night. When nobody voiced out an answer, he took the suggestion back and sent them all home.

Isabel West received her brother with a smile when he arrived that night.

"What is that smile you are wearing?" Wilfred stared at her with a dreadful face.

"I have a feeling—"

He cut her. "Good for you to have one."

"Do you not want to know?"

"Know what?"

"Kristova and Coldwell Mansions are brewing their second house war."

Wilfred was aware that Isabel would be the first person to be happy if that eventuality would occur. And since he had enough of her and her shenanigans, he only mumbled, "I will gladly die in it."

"How Juliet of you!"

"Better be Juliet than to be a bitter aftertaste like you, Isabel."

She was enraged at that. "Why do you hate me so?!"

"You do not know?!" he hollered back. Only his side was facing the ill figure of a woman.

"Have the courage to tell me, Lord West! For courage is something you never had."

Wilfred turned to her, faced her, eyes to eyes. "And you think you are courageous enough? You hate to admit that you detest both houses because your envy is as vast as the sea."

"What the hell?!"

"Why are you trying to please people you never liked? To give validity to your existence?"

"Shame on you! I have a purpose, and you do not!"

"You despise Madam Kristova. I get it. She is unapologetically not trying to please anybody. And you fear because the moment that you show your truest colors you will lose admirers when she still has hers."

Isabel's tears were falling from her eyes.

"And you hate Sir Coldwell because you were unable to capture his heart when in fact you are the most qualified noblewoman in the capital after the youngest princess."

"That man is hexed!"

"Do you really think I will never know about your sly tricks on Elric? But the man is too kind to talk behind your back or speak anything evil against you. Because you are my sister!"

"I loathe you, Lord West!"

"And I loathe this family," he barked, "this family that turned you into numb, unfeeling, and lonely. Why are you so afraid to leave this rotten house? You deserve freedom from this bridewell they raised you in. Give liberty to your wrists from the long suffering, from the shackles of duty to family." And he begged, "It is time to save yourself, too, dearest sister."

"Easy for you to say. You are a man, you are a lord. You can do anything, everything you desire. And I? What do I possess? I own nothing, even my own heart."

"They prayed for your birth, did they not?"

"What do you even mean?"

"Did they pray for your birth or not?"

"They did!"

"That only means you were yours before you became theirs."

Wilfred exited the scene and climbed to his room. Isabel then carried her weary heart, took the carriage, and headed towards the queen's palace.

Chapter Eighteen

The two houses which remained at war with each other busied themselves about the future and arranged marriages were of no exemption.

Edward Coldwell decided for his nephew to join the trading industry since it was what Elric had studied in the King's University. They discussed such a topic over dinner once and Elric agreed with him without trying to debate on the matter. Edward did not doubt his nephew's decision and was glad that the young man was finally thinking logically.

House Coldwell started meeting other houses which made Elric mostly preoccupied for the whole get-together, as they called it. He only saw Antonia's image even though he was facing another house's lady or miss. He could not imagine himself being married to someone he never loved and doing things he never wanted to do. He even often prayed for Ship Maharlika to show up at once, since he had no other plans if the ship would not dock in the capital's port anymore. Ship Maharlika was the sole plan, and it was coming late, two weeks late.

One of the houses they agreed to meet with was House Grimaldi. The madam of the house was rich but the younger lady she was with came from Gravin, whose name bore Huntington. Sir Coldwell, after knowing about the lady's homeland and bloodline, did not proceed with the promised meetings and stood the women up. He had guessed correctly that Miss Lyona was from a poor family and only clung to Madam Grimaldi to find herself a rich man in the capital to marry.

But fate was not blind to Sir Coldwell's deliberate act of offense. When he received the news about House Renaldi's tragedy, both of its lord and heir met their demise, he sent a letter to ask for a visitation. Miss Renaldi, the remaining family and bereaved daughter of the house, honestly replied that she was not allowing his house for a visit. Her reasons were not stated but Sir Coldwell expected it was because she was Madam Kristova's godchild.

Maria Kristova, too, planned things for her granddaughters. She urged Katarin to accept Isabel West's invitation regarding organizing the other Great Nine balls since she loved planning and managing events. Katarin felt content on the topic. The madam suggested Antonia to continue doing something at the monastery. She did not allow her to frequent the capital's library anymore because she had a feeling the young Coldwell was also an ink drinker.

Katarin and Antonia both received suitors as well. All were not from the capital but all were of high stature in Gravin and Primus. And all were rich and handsome, too. However, all never liked the twins after knowing their not so ordinary interests. The former loved Witchery while the latter loved Winery.

Two brothers visited them one time, James and Henry. Both were born in Gravin but brought up in Hert. And they were one of the most sought bachelors in the country. The twins liked the brothers at first. But their boastful nature was a turnoff. And so, they never gained the twin hearts.

Antonia felt pleased at the thought of not being liked by their suitors in the end.

Katarin was worried, though. She was three-and-twenty and suitable for marriage. She was confused why it was difficult for others to accept her odd interests. She was viewed by the public as a perfect wife material, only if she was not into incantations and spells. But she could never get rid of her love for Witchery. It was just about honoring nature and thanking it for its bounty.

"Why did you not marry, Aunt Maria?" Antonia had the audacity to ask the madam while they were attending a private ball.

The older woman held her wine and raised it to her. "Because I am content with my life."

"She is lying," said a stranger who invited herself to their table. Elisa Pierce was touched after hearing from Richard Kovalski about how Madam Kristova's revelation on their kinship silenced her issue with Antonia. And she could not help herself express her gratitude in person when she saw the three. "Good evening!"

Madam Kristova, to her surprise, stood and hugged Elisa. "Please, come home."

"And stain your beautiful image?"

"You cannot stain an already ruined image, my dear." Both laughed at the thought.

"Thank you for everything, Aunt Maria."

"Just come home. I will be relieved."

Katarin and Antonia followed and hugged Elisa as well. It was then that Elisa Pierce was publicly accepted as a Kristova.

"Now, are we not a party of odd ladies?" Antonia murmured.

"Indeed," Katarin giggled. "And the public hate that we are happy and content with ourselves."

"But as long as we know our truth, the public will not matter." Elisa poured herself wine.

"It seems I raised you well, girls. I raised you well." Madam Kristova commented as she raised her glass. "Cheers!"

"So, why are you not married again?" Elisa interrupted.

"Because the public said I poisoned the man I was soon to marry." The madam beamed. "And since then, men have been afraid to get near me."

"I still love that version of the story."

But Antonia was not satisfied. "What is the real version then?"

"If given the right to tell the real version of the story, I will be honored to breathe life to it." Lili Crossman joined their table, with her was Diana Constantin. "I forgot to bring Isabel West," she jested.

"Are we going to learn about the real version now?" Katarin was curious as well.

"Should I?" Lili referred to Maria, earning her a positive response, considering names would be concealed. "A is Aunt Maria, B is the best friend and the dead man, C is the cousin of that dead man. We cannot name names because we are in public, though this is a private ball. You get me, yes?"

Everyone nodded.

"A and B met first but A fell in love with C. End of story."

"Aunt Lili is a tease," grumbled Katarin.

Antonia grabbed the chance to continue the story. "It was a love triangle. B loved A, A loved C, C loved A but C loved B more than A. When B died, A and C blamed each other. And instead of loving each other, they hated each other. Yet hate is still love, love that cannot be contained and has nowhere to go. Both ended up not wanting the love they have for the other."

"And you did not marry because of this?" Diana turned to Maria.

"I was grieving for two decades, D," Maria smiled, "and the next thing I know, I am too old to marry."

"Pity! I still want to find a husband at this age. Are you, Lili?"

"I don't know. I was never attracted to one."

"Are you into women?"

"I mean I was never attracted to anyone."

Elisa teased, "Anyone curious how to make babies?" earning her a mixture of looks from her companions. Antonia smiled sourly, Katarin closed her eyes, Diana raised a brow, Lili reddened, and Maria looked terrified. "I am jesting. It is my job to put smiles on your faces. You spinsters are so serious!"

"Good heavens! I begin to love the spinster's table," humored Katarin.

"Agreed," Antonia seconded. "Told you it is fun to be a spinster."

"If you are not alone being one," countered Elisa.

But Diana put a halt on their merriment. "Until you are sixty summers and must become a nun to be kept in the mountains."

"What?!" chorused the others.

"You did not know?" Diana barked at them. "No wonder. You are not from here after all."

"I will die before I reach sixty," was what all Antonia said, her heart filled with resistance. The others emptied their wine glasses in revolt.

Chapter Nineteen

One dawn, outside Elisa's window, the street dwellers were in a commotion. She heard people shouting out of excitement. She only sat up from bed when she comprehended that a huge ship had docked at the capital port.

A clearer announcement was shouted aloud, stating, "Ship Maharlika is here!" making Elisa jump from her bed to see outside her window. And there it was, Ship Maharlika in all its glory. With its arrival it kindled hearts which were on the verge of retreating to its deepest core and hiding there forever.

Despite her good relation with Kristova Mansion recently, Elisa stood her ground and decided to board the ship where she hoped a different life awaited her. She then pulled a bag from under her bed with all the things she prepared for her journey when there was a sudden knock on her door.

Elisa opened the door to Richard Kovalski. Though he was the one who helped her regarding her employment on that ship, she had to wave him good bye and free her heart from its fancy.

"She is here," he said, referring to Ship Maharlika.

"I know. I've heard. I'm ready."

"Shall we?"

"Are you coming?"

Richard's heart was wavering. He did not want Elisa to go, but he must let her go. If he could never fight for her, if he could not go with her, he should at least give her the life she deserved even when he would never be a part of it anymore. "No." He did not need to explain it to her. She understood. "But I will escort you to meet Mr Qalif."

Elisa nodded. "Thank you for this, for taking care of me, for everything."

"If I cannot save myself, Elisa, saving you will mean a lot to me."

The thought pained Elisa. Richard was suffering just as she was. Both wanted to change their fates but he had a family, a house, to keep. Unlike her, she had nothing to lose.

"Richard," she whispered, "what did I do to deserve this part of you?"

"You have been the sunshine during darkest years of my life. I want you to go on living and giving light to others. You deserve more than this country. You deserve everything."

Elisa cried at his revelation that in exchange she grabbed his collar, tiptoed and kissed him passionately. Richard accepted what was given to him and was lost in the process. It was what he longed for, the tenderness of her kiss and her loving touch.

When Elisa let go from the intimate scene, Richard hugged her tight in order for time to stand still. "I hope you won't change your mind about me," she said softly. "I am no woman with an easy virtue. Forgive me for kissing you, I just felt like I needed to."

If there was any change of mind, Richard adored Elisa more than ever. "Take good care of yourself now," he returned. "And please be happy."

Elric Coldwell was grateful at the news of Ship Maharlika's arrival. He was finally going to achieve his dream of owning his life. He packed a few things and left the Coldwell Mansion without a trace. Even the letters written by Antonia which he used to keep and read over and over all jumped into the fire. At the docks he saw the ship of his dreams, and without having any second thoughts he went aboard. The first he searched for when he was on it was Antonia. But her face did not grace the crowd yet.

Antonia Kristova, after a long time, was in a man's garments again. She escaped the Kristova Mansion without bringing any clothes to avoid suspicions from everyone. She loved Kristova Mansion, even the newly created spinster's table, but she wanted to try another version of her story. She wanted to travel and taste all the wine in the world. The sight of Ship Maharlika amazed her and as soon as she went up the ship, the employer was calling the qualified names for employment. Her name was called. Elric's too.

"I thought you changed your mind," Elric whispered in Antonia's ears the moment he was beside her.

"I am sorry for making you think that way. It was difficult to leave home."

"We got the employment."

"Yes, I have heard. Congrats!"

"Cheers to us!"

Wilfred West, too, boarded the ship, without telling anyone, and as a guest. He was in a trance. He never met a princess in his life. That was his only chance. He wanted to meet the Arab royalty before her ship left the capital's dock.

"The last one is Elisa Pierce. Those who were not mentioned can get off the ship if you were here for employment alone," said Mr Qalif, as Wilfred saw him in the middle of the crowd. And above him was a beautiful woman in an extravagant royal blue attire decorated with diamonds. She had a red gem on her forehead and a golden nose ring, too. Her hands were sketched with flowers and her wrists were clad with golden bracelets.

When the crowd cleared the way, Wilfred was already walking towards the beauty whom he believed to be the Arab princess he dreamt of seeing. And he was captivated at the sight the moment he saw her, as he expected. Such beauty was unique and heavenly. He wanted to leave after seeing the royalty but something in him was not convinced to do so. Thus, he stood there watching, waiting. As she smiled he was trapped in the haze he did not want to escape from. She was too mysterious, particularly with the language he had no knowledge of. Wilfred wore his tender curiosity on his sleeve and nothing could satiate it but an honest encounter. He was never loyal to his women, because he knew they only wanted to control him because of his rank in the capital. But this Arab royalty had him in her palms in just one sight. And he found himself wishing for the princess to not be married yet nor even betrothed, though he was certain he had no chance to be one of her prospects at all.

The Arab princess finally noticed Wilfred when they both felt the tremors below the deck. Everyone stood still though their minds were anxious. And before all the tables turned to materialize the dreams of everybody, Ship Maharlika unexpectedly blew up and was sliced in two. Together with its explosion were the aspirations and dreams of those who already hoped and expected so much.

That year Ship Maharlika was written in the history of Simetra as "The Ship That Never Sailed."

Chapter Twenty

Maria Kristova opened a letter from Rudolf that morning and she was taken aback by the contents of the letter.

Dearest Aunt Maria,

How is everything? I am alive and well. The war ended and I am grateful to you for taking good care of my family. Juliet said you took my girls to the training school to protect them from war. I know Antonia hated the idea but I thank you for doing so. I met a young Coldwell in the garrison and before he left the south he helped me restore my home. He is a good man. Juliet said Antonia and he are friends. I hope you will allow the connection. And I do pray you'll forgive the master of House Coldwell for blaming you on your best friend's death who was also his dear cousin. It is for your own peace of mind.

Aunt, I hope that you will let our Antonia love the young Coldwell if she loves him. If Elric does not deserve our Antonia, let them both realize it. He did not tell me about it but I am aware of his fondness towards her. He said they will meet at the docks but they will not elope. Let them go.

Anyhow, I will be waiting for my twin daughters here in our hometown with Juliet beside me when they are ready. Even though I want to pay you a visit in the capital, I need to do final repairs in my home. I look forward to your reply.

Please, be well.

Your nephew,

Rudolf

The letter made Madam Kristova think things over until she saw her adversary outside her window. Edward Coldwell marched towards Kristova Mansion without minding the explosion at the docks. He was knocking with all his energy at the door until Madam Kristova, who was also enraged, opened it.

"How dare you come knocking at my doors?!" she hollered as if she opened the portal for the devil.

"You witches!" he grunted. "Your granddaughter seduced my nephew!" Edward then handed a letter written by Antonia. He saw it earlier in the fireplace at Elric's room, partly burned, bearing Antonia's name. By then he realized it was her who posed as Antoine Noir.

"Who seduced who?" Maria hurled. "My nephew in Ardia sent me a letter, bringing news about Elric's affection towards my Antonia. He is in love with her!"

"Impossible! In love? Where is Elric?!"

"He is not here!"

"Show me your granddaughter then!" Edward entered Maria's house without her permission.

"You, ugly toad! This is trespassing! This is harassment!"

"And who is that?" Edward glared at Katarin who just went down the stairs.

"Can't you recall? She is the twin sister?"

"Aunt Maria, Antonia is not in her room," Katarin informed not just her great-aunt but everyone in the entrance hall.

"What's happening?" Lili cried out of confusion and worry.

Another explosion occurred, shaking the capital, and took everyone's attention inside Kristova Mansion. All of them went running outside and witnessed a big ball of dark cloud in the sky somewhere at the port.

"Oh, my goodness!" Maria gasped. "Don't tell me they are on that ship." She was reminded by Rudolf's letter. Elric and Antonia were to meet at the docks.

Edward only glanced with woeful eyes at Maria, the woman he solely loved but had to give up because his cousin would be heartbroken, before leaving and heading for the port. Maria tailed after him. Lili and Katarin were running behind them as well.

The outcome of the explosion wiped out the whole port. Black mist covered the entire area and bodies were lying everywhere. Smaller boats were broken into pieces, wooden scraps were scattered and the bawls of women were audible from afar.

Edward Coldwell and Maria Kristova could not believe what happened and what their eyes had seen in the port from a distance. Perhaps the war did not absolutely end. And both the master and the madam of the houses which were in blood feud for years stood frozen after hearing from one of the passersby that a Coldwell and a Kristova were on the ship for an employment.

Maria's knees weakened and fell to the ground. Yet Edward caught her before she completely collapsed.

"This is not what I have wanted to happen, Edward. This is not the one."

"I know, I know. It's not your fault, Maria."

"But it is. I have been so overbearing."

"If you believe so, I will share the burden. I tried to control Elric, too."

"What have we done, Eddie? We did it again. And this time, two dear ones lost their lives."

"Oh, Mary, forgive me."

"Forgive me, too."

That moment, the two houses unexpectedly reunited to share the burden of losing, though not yet confirmed, two cherished beings. Lili Crossman hugged Katarin Kristova tightly after realizing what just transpired, and they cried together.

After hearing the news, Diana Constantin appeared at Kristova Mansion to console her friends, only to see that Edward and Maria were already battling such a burden side by side. She felt glad for them reconnecting but heartbroken still for the happenstance needed so the act would be done.

Isabel West set foot on Kristova Mansion too, when the sad news reached her. She had a feeling Wilfred was on that ship together with his friends. Richard's family blamed her brother for dragging him to be on that ship. It was the decision he made on his letter for Richard which landed in the hands of his father.

"Maria, I am so sorry for everything I have caused you," Isabel confessed which earned a warm hug from the madam.

"Was Wilfred out there too?"

"Yes, according to whisperers. And Richard Kovalski."

The women inside the drawing room began to cry again.

"Oh, heavens! Have mercy!"

"Elisa was there too."

Katarin wailed. It seemed most of the people she loved in the capital were so eager to be on that ship and flee Simetra. She understood the women but could not reason out for the men.

"This is my fault," Edward Coldwell said. "I always wanted to control Elric's life even though I could not control mine. But he is my only family and I did not want him gone. I feel so alone, for years, with no friends or relatives to turn to. And I did not want him leave me which resulted to this, his eagerness to leave me."

"I told Wilfred he lacked purpose," Isabel then shared. "Maybe he thought to find it on the ship. And for Richard, we all know how the Kovalskis were to their sons, like how the Wests were to their daughters. It was why Tristan died back then, he poisoned himself to find liberty, and why Juliet eloped to escape an arranged matrimony. And Ship Maharlika was the poison they all chose this time."

"Tristan did not poison himself," corrected Maria. "The moonflower was mine."

Edward added, "His worries about his family killed him."

"I was willing to marry Tristan back then. But he died before my answer reached him."

Lili's eyes were swelling, Katarin's too. Isabel and Diana could not believe what they discovered that night.

Chapter Twenty-One

Scavengers searched the port for survivors by midnight after securing no more explosives were planted in the area. Ship Maharlika separated in two and was burned to the ground, ceasing Expedition VII.

A member of the search party found a ring with a blue stone on a finger of someone's hand whom he thought was a corpse. He seized the ring and to his surprise the finger moved, refusing to surrender the treasure. The man yielded and pulled the scraps of wood which covered the body and shouted, "The princess is alive!"

When Wilfred West woke up, he was already at the hospital. The things he remembered were only a little. He had in his mind a vision of him dragging the Arab princess down the ship before the second explosion. He believed himself to be too gutless to die for another person, but there he was in a hospital bed after being dauntless.

Not far from his bed, five bodies were lying—an old man, a gentleman and three ladies. The old man was identified as Mr Qalif, the owner of the office where they were found. The office, a combination of iron and steel as its exterior and with wood as its interior as Mr Qalif designed it, saved them from certain death. Wilfred remembered seeing Richard Kovalski's figure calling him while he was holding the royalty's hand to escape the terror.

Wilfred was then surprised to see Antonia and Elisa in the same hall with him.

"Antonia, what were you thinking?" Wilfred asked his niece when he went near her the moment she was conscious.

"I was accepted as a journalist. I wanted to own my life, uncle."

"Who were you with?"

"I was with—" but Antonia did not see Elric in the hall and decided to keep it a secret, "no one." She looked at Wilfred, confused by the terrible occurrence on the ship and inside her heart. She was worried about not seeing Elric when in fact they were together inside Mr Qalif's office before the entire ship blew up. She then began crying at the thought of Elric dying. And it was her fault. She initiated the plan.

Richard and Elisa shocked Wilfred the most. They were kissing in front of everyone when they got near each other. He never noticed his friend admiring the woman in the past. When he heard Richard saying, "I will never let you go, Elisa. I have loved you since then and I'll never give you up," he was puzzled all the more.

Wilfred was confused with everything he just witnessed. Antonia was trying to leave the capital and

Richard loved Elisa. Yet what surprised him more was when the Arab princess stood before him. He faced her and she still looked angelic despite the dust which scattered over her body.

"You saved me," spoke the princess with her hands in motion, corresponding to every word for him to comprehend her. "I thank you."

"It's an honor, princess," he replied.

"In me country, when you save me, me is yours."

Wilfred gasped at what he heard. "I don't understand."

"I marry you."

"But I am not wealthy, I am no prince."

"Heart," said the princess, touching Wilfred's chest, "more value, not gold."

Wilfred lost his mind at the royalty's words. Everything was happening too fast. Later Mr Qalif was talking to the Arab princess using a language Wilfred did not understand. The next time she talked to him, she gave him the ring with a blue stone which was the symbol of her being the Arab princess. Mr Qalif translated the woman's promise and said, "She will be back for you and that ring is proof of her return."

"Can you ask her for her name?" Wilfred asked.

"Safiya," the Arab princess replied before leaving the hospital and the people who saved her from sure death.

Wilfred West couldn't imagine it. He was going to marry the princess he only wanted to see in the first place. In just a day he found the love of his life and the one he would be marrying soon. He couldn't believe he'd be a victim of love at all. He was too happy even when he went home and informed his family he's marrying an Arab princess. His family was grateful he was safe and his decision of getting married was not questionable for he was actually pretty late in terms of settling down and by that creating his own family. He was needed to produce a successor for West Mansion too. Isabel West was relieved to have her brother back.

Elisa Pierce was hopeful. She did not need to leave the capital anymore. She had a reason to stay and it was Richard, the man she loved ever since she laid eyes on him. She wasn't wrong at all for assuming that he loved her. And that was because he had been helping her, caring for her and protecting her. Though he had many women, only one could have his heart and that was her. She was glad she was alive to witness the day Richard confessed he loved her too.

Richard Kovalski was full of courage. He survived the explosion, he would survive his kin's judgement. He was done saving everyone. He deserved his own saving. And he had every right to choose whom to marry and be with for the rest of his days. He never wanted to be rich. He only wanted to be happy.

And with Elisa, he knew very well he would be. So he brought her with him home. He told his parents he was marrying her even if they would never agree. His parents did not object which did not surprise him and that was because he said he did not want to end up like his Uncle Tristan. Elisa introduced herself as a Kristova that moment, too, adding more hatred towards her by Richard's parents. But the son willfully decided and even if they did not like it, acceptance was the best option to move forward and for the elders to earn peace. Finally, it was peace they were aiming for and not the highest class or rank in the capital.

Antonia Kristova felt guilty, however, when a nurse informed them that Elric Coldwell was sent to a solitary room for further observation. The man lost his sense of sight and did not accept any visitors but his uncle. As a result, Antonia needed to leave the hospital without seeing nor saying good bye to Elric which devastated her so much. She blamed herself for his misfortune. If she wasn't so mischievous, they would never be there at all and Elric could still see. And she was angry at herself for taking Elric along with her, dreaming of owning a life she thought they'd finally have. And look where it brought them. So even the moment she went back to her hometown with her twin, she still had a regretful heart.

Elric Coldwell was guilty, too. He was older than Antonia, but he never acted his age. He was childish to think he could have a life he always wanted. He did a lot of introspection after the explosion and losing his sight made him decide to avoid Antonia from then on. Getting close to her led them to this, much more could happen if he would remain stubborn. He was thankful he only lost his sense of sight and not the life of his beloved Antonia. If he lost her, he would die every day for the rest of his life. Losing his sight was enough punishment for trying to deviate from duty to family, and with it he would forever repent.

The explosion made a change inside people's cores. Some became brave. Some caved in. Some reconciled. However, all required the same dosage of courage to do what must be done. For love, for peace.

Chapter Twenty-Two

For six months Antonia redirected her energy to her father's vineyard. She had been blaming herself about Elric's situation, believing he forever lost his sense of sight. She sent him letters in the earlier months but she received no reply from them. And with it she thought the man was angry at her for the comeuppance of their plan.

When their house received wedding invitations from both Wilfred and Elisa one day, they talked about going but Antonia decided to not attend such a happy occasion. She was afraid to see Elric and be blamed by his sufferings, considering he deliberately ignored her. No news of him regaining his sight had reached her, thus she was guilty more and more every day. However, she changed her resolve when she realized how much she loved and cared about Elric. She was willing to atone for her mistakes and be punished by serving him at his house, if given the chance.

Wilfred West was the first who got married. The Arab princess, Safiya, arrived one day, boarding a ship full of gold and her servants. She had her parents' blessing to wed the man who saved her life. Isabel West became very close with her as soon as they met.

Princess Safiya insisted on living in a simple way, compared to her luxurious life in the Arab kingdom, as long as she was with Wilfred and his family at the West Mansion. That was why their church wedding was quite simple as well. She wore a white wedding dress and appeared like a nymph despite its simplicity.

The flower ladies were Antonia and Katarin. Lili Crossman and Diana Constantin had the privilege to hold the candles. Isabel West was the best woman, Mr Ramini Qalif was the man of honor. The bridesmaids were Elisa and Juliet Kristova, and the groomsmen were Richard Kovalski and Rudolf Kristov. Sir Edward Coldwell was the ring bearer while Maria Kristova held the band, the fabric of unity.

After the wedding, Sir Edward did not proceed to the reception. He retired early and gave no information about his nephew. Coldwell Mansion was too tight-lipped that even the public bore no news if Elric was forever blind.

Antonia halfheartedly enjoyed the rest of the wedding. All she thought of was Elric whom she could not feel the existence anymore. It was as if he disappeared with no trace. Nobody talked about him, nobody tried to. And it devastated her in every way.

Richard Kovalski and Elisa Pierce got married next. It was a garden wedding by sundown. There were no roles to play but the bride and groom. The rest of the attendees were all witnesses. Everyone they loved were there, except for Elric still.

The reception occurred later at nighttime. Candles lit the gardens of Kristova Mansion. People were jovial and filled with bliss. But Antonia's mind was somewhere else. It had been preoccupied ever since the explosion. Nothing could ease her, not the sweetest cake nor the finest wine. To be the cause why Elric isolated himself from everyone was too much to bear, yet she could not help to be guilty of everything.

Mr and Mrs Kovalski received an excessive gift from Princess Safiya which made them rich enough to climb up the elite class. The couple was able to buy the capital's theater because of what the princess gave and restored the building to its former glory. Entertaining people officially became their business and they finally earned their respect from society.

Katarin Kristova decided on settling in the capital after the weddings. She accepted Isabel West's proposal to organize balls together. She thought to never find love and busied herself with managing events and socializing with noblemen, foreigners too.

Antonia decided to go home with her parents. She longed for the vineyards and the trees, her horses too. If Elric did not want her, she had to move on. Her father's land awaits, the rivers and streams were to die for, and her books needed reading. She was excited to leave the capital and be home. She missed her cats too.

The first thing that Rudolf Kristov did when he was back home, after a three-day trip, was to do a few rounds in his vineyard. Antonia was his assistant in doing so.

"Shall we talk about him?" asked the father.

"Elric?"

He nodded.

"Can I not refuse?"

"I think it is time to discuss it."

"Papa, I am fine."

"Let us play a game," he suggested. "Whoever gets to the stable first, wins. If I win, you talk. If you win, we drink."

"Okay." But Rudolf already started as she said so, earning him a shout from her. "What a cheat!"

"So?" the father asked, smiling, as Antonia reached the stable the last.

"I hate you," she grumbled. "We talk, we drink."

"Much better."

Rudolf and Antonia found themselves at the fireplace with a wine between them and a piece of meat Juliet prepared for them. After a few glasses, Antonia shared about everything. Not just Elric but also about the world and the capital's standard on women.

"Hert was too much for me. I did not belong there. The rules were suffocating. Girls must wear dresses, not drinking, must be suitable for marriage, bla bla bla. Elric was the same. He must be successful enough to be the next lord of his house, must be in the trading business, must be congenial to meet a wife.

Heavens, arranged marriages was a must. Unlike us Ardians, we die alone if we must than beg for love. I wanted to escape with Elric on that ship. I will write, he will draw. It was dreamy. But it exploded before our dreams were realized. I worry about him so much."

"If I knew, I should have brought you to the garrisons than sent you to the capital," teased Rudolf.

Antonia laughed. "I wonder how Aunt Maria survived the capital for so long. It is a terrible place for odd people like us."

"Glad I was born and raised in Ardia. It is a place with no judgement as long as you do no harm to trees and animals."

"I know."

"You really love Elric that much?"

"Do you know how weird it is to talk about the man I love with my father over wine?"

"Lad, I know him. I was his commanding officer in the garrison."

"No way!"

"He was called Erradyn."

"Really, Captain Kallistar?"

"Indeed," Rudolf smiled. "And if you want to know, he helped me restore this house. But he does not know you are my child."

"Did you not tell him?"

"He did not ask."

"What a cheat!"

"He loves you, I know."

Antonia felt like crying.

"He said he will meet you at the docks. I asked if you were eloping but he said it was not the plan. He loves you enough to never do that to you."

"Father, I am the reason why he is blind."

"Don't blame yourself, lad."

"He does not reply to my letters."

"Keep waiting, lad," Rudolf insisted. "Did you not say he is blind? How can he write back?"

Antonia rolled her eyes. She did not think of that, and he was right. "Oh, heavens!" She then cried more.

"What now?"

"He is blind. Elric not writing back only means he is blind until this very moment. Oh, heavens! Oh, no!" She hugged her thick blanket and sobbed. She was dizzy from the wine and later had fallen asleep.

Chapter Twenty-Three

Sir Edward Coldwell, together with an eye doctor, found his nephew in the terrace of his bedroom. He was sitting on a chair, beside him was a table with coffee and many letters on it.

"Elric?" the uncle called. "The doctor is here."

"Good morning!" the nephew greeted as he palmed the table to stand. "Please, take a seat."

The doctor inquired if the sun was not blinding for Elric, he said it was not. It was even soothing to him like a warm hug from a friend.

"How are you?"

"I am not totally blind anymore, doctor," Elric informed. "I woke up this morning seeing everything again."

"That is good news, Elric." Sir Edward finally felt at ease after a very long time. His nephew could see again.

"But the colors I see are limited."

"What are those?"

"I see white, black, grey, and every shade of red." Red. Elric hated red when he was a boy. He used to think it was the color of pain because every time he saw blood it was pain he could feel. But after meeting

Antonia and seeing her red hair, his hate for red changed into adoration and bravery. He never expected that somewhere in time he would love the color red. And now it was the only vibrant color he could see. He could also determine the other shades of it.

"I am afraid," the doctor admitted, "that this is the finality of your condition. In most cases, patients remained totally blind, or could see only in black and white."

"We should be thankful then, doctor, should we not?" said Sir Edward.

"Compared to total blindness, we should be."

"Thank you, doctor, for all your help." Elric then escorted the doctor towards the door of Coldwell Mansion.

Sir Edward Coldwell on one hand, before leaving the room, checked the letters on Elric's table and saw Antonia's name, as the sender, in all of it. After months of being shelved, Elric was finally able to read them. He insisted to read it himself, believing he could see again and never giving up in doing so.

"What do you want to do first?" asked Sir Edward when he met Elric at the stairs.

"I will visit my friends."

"Shall I accompany you?"

"No, uncle. You have been with me for so long. Even since I was a boy as I remember. What I wish for is for you to visit Madam Kristova. Your bad blood is over, yes?"

"Are you sure you will be fine on your own?"

"Of course."

Elric Coldwell visited Wilfred West after sending a letter to Richard Kovalski to meet him at the West Mansion. The three men gathered again but this time it was only Elric who had no woman on his side.

"Forgive me for not being able to attend your weddings. I did not want to break a glass or anything." Elric gave a laugh at the thought.

Richard cleared his throat. "Health is the utmost priority."

"Forgive us too if we were so eager to get married." Wilfred forced a smile.

Elric grinned. "Don't worry, I understand. I would have done the same."

Princess Safiya investigated more about Elric's eyes and they discovered he was colorblind. "I see red though," he added.

"Antonia was at our weddings," Elisa mentioned, beaming. "But she seemed lost most of the time. Are you going to visit her too? Too bad she went back to Ardia already."

Richard tried to stop his wife from talking more by squeezing her hand. But she kept on talking, "They are in Mayari, if you want to know."

Wilfred then noticed, "Why visit Antonia?"

"You do not know?" Elisa raised her brows.

"Well, what is there to know?" Wilfred's eyes travelled from Elisa to Richard and back.

Elisa shrugged. "Elric and Antonia?"

"What is with them?" Wilfred eyed Elric.

Princess Safiya whispered to her husband about it and he brightened. "Antonia? She was the one dressed as a man? She was the woman in black?"

"I love her, yes," Elric confessed, his eyes moist. And in his revelation, there was an underlying sadness. "God, I love her so much."

Wilfred appeared too elated at the news. He was supportive of it. "When are you going to propose?"

Elric combed his hair with his fingers. "Oh, good heavens!"

"I do not think he is going to propose," Richard thought.

"Why not?!" chorused Elisa and Wilfred.

"Because he is afraid."

"Afraid of what?!" Elisa and Wilfred said in unison again.

"She stopped writing to me." Elric sniffed, the tears in his eyes signified defeat.

"Just go to her and tell her what you feel," suggested Richard. "Or write a reply to her letters. It is about time."

"Don't allow your guilt to eat you, Elric," was what Princess Safiya uttered. "If you love her, be with her before it is too late. Stop imagining or believing things you are not certain about."

Elisa was stressed out upon watching Elric succumbing to his fears. "Don't you get it? Antonia loves you. What more do you want to know?"

Richard hugged his wife. "Honey, Elric here is traumatized by the explosion. He is now fearful to be with Antonia because he feels like he is the reason why she almost died. He does not want to be the reason why anyone dies."

"Is your love not greater than your fear?" asked Princess Safiya.

Elisa added, "The bombing was caused by the machinery below the ship. Nothing else."

"Elric thinks he tolerated Antonia. If he acted as an adult for the two of them they would not be on that boat in the first place."

"We were all there, were we not? And we are all well. Look at me now, I am an elephant." Elisa brought back the laughter to their small get-together.

Richard kissed her. "Take that back. You are no elephant."

"I am sorry. It was not a good joke."

"It is an honor to keep your jokes in check, my love."

"Oh, Richard!"

"I love you both," Richard said as he held her protruding belly with their baby.

"Get a room!" barked Wilfred while lacing his hand with Princess Safiya's.

Elric was glad to witness his friends happy in the arms of their women. And it was true love, not arranged. Elric was only allowed to leave after having an evening meal with them. Despite their excitement, Elisa and Wilfred were warned by Richard to not meddle with Elric's tribulation, particularly if they planned to write a letter to Ardia bearing the good news on Elric's health. Princess Safiya agreed and sided with Richard. Some battles must be fought and won on its own.

Chapter Twenty-Four

A man and a woman met again after a long time to resolve a matter they had begun. But before that fateful day, the woman received a letter from the man three days prior.

My Mary,

I haven't told you this, but I must, even if it is too late. That night before Tristan died, he made a confession that you are to turn down his proposal. But he warned me to never blame you if he wouldn't live to witness the next day. And that he will understand your decision for he was aware of your affection towards me. His parents had been pressuring him to climb up the elite status through you, but he did not have the heart to betray you more than he ever did. It seemed death was his only chance to escape and have peace though the detective said otherwise.

Unfortunately, I got offended after you told me I should have been watching him keenly. That's why I told you the words which I have been regretting since the day I uttered them, even until this time. I know I have hurt you and I am so sorry for only telling you this time what I should have told you before everything got worse. I tried, I swear I tried but subtly. I should have told you directly but I was too late. You were absolutely mad at me.

But I love you, Mary. Only you. I was very fearful and I punished myself for making your heart choose me when it was Tristan who met you first and knew you well. Tristan was my dear cousin and was a brother to me. I couldn't hurt him. And forgive me if not hurting him and punishing myself made you the victim. Yet you have my heart ever since. In between the then and the now, and forever I'll be—

Yours,

Eddie

"I have heard that you are now alone in that house," stated Edward Coldwell beside Maria Kristova. They were at a park, sitting close but not close enough to be mistaken as a couple.

"I disagree with you on that, old man. Last time I checked I still have my maidservants with me."

"You'll never change, won't you, Mary?"

Maria smirked. "No. You cannot teach new tricks to an old dog, Eddie. But I am afraid we can never be more than friends in this lifetime."

"I respect your decision," Edward uttered though he was pained by what Maria just said. "Still, I am happy our houses are in good relations again, with each other."

"I know. It's been two decades, I presume."

"Two decades long. And we are old for something childish, don't you think?"

"Agreed," Maria looked at the heavens. "Now tell me. How's your nephew doing?"

"I pity him. His soul left him since that horrible day."

"Poor thing! Did he not regain his sight at all?"

"That's what we thought but he had it back. However, he is now colorblind."

"Goodness!" Maria sighed. "Yet we can be grateful he can see again."

"Yes, in a way. And how about your granddaughter?"

"Antonia never wrote to me anymore. I think she's blaming herself for what happened to your nephew. She actually never stopped feeling guilty and devastated when they left the capital for Ardia. And when she came here to witness Wilfred's wedding, as well as Elisa's, she looked forever lonely."

"I believe this is all our fault. And now, they are letting something beautiful slip away from their fingers."

"What do you think we can do?"

"I think I know the answer to that."

"Is it much better than mine?"

"Why did you ask in the first place then?"

"To make sure you're still using your brain."

"You're still a witch for that."

"Said the ever-arrogant frog."

"That you were in love with once upon a time."

"Oh, quit it, I say!"

Edward laughed. Maria smiled. They might not have had the chance to be lovers in this story but their friendship became stronger than in the past. There was more teasing and laughing and affection.

"Shall we do a regroup on Saturdays again? Just like the olden days, but this time with Diana and Isabel."

"I love the idea, Eddie," Maria grinned. "You think Isabel is still obsessed with you?"

"I hope she is not."

"I heard she is into foreigners lately, with the swarm of tourists arriving at the capital port."

"I think we should do the same, Mary."

Maria laughed. "No, thank you."

"Are you not afraid?"

"Of what?"

"To be a nun in the mountains when you reach sixty. You have what, ten or eleven years left?"

"Ha! Do not be troubled. I can always go back to Ardia. However, being a nun in the mountains is not a bad ending."

"Don't be ridiculous, Mary."

"If you worry so much, hex me to ask your hand in marriage before I turn sixty."

Edward Coldwell wanted to leap at the idea. "Never deny your words when the time comes."

"I will not. But the question is, can you put a spell on me?"

"I have at least ten years to try. Do not challenge me."

"And I thought we are too old for childish things," Maria reminded both of them.

"We are never too old for anything."

Maria suddenly suggested. "Should we visit Tristan?"

"Is that what you want?"

"Yes."

"Then let us take Lili as well."

"Much better."

Tristan Kovalski's headstone remained clean despite the many years he passed away. His friends and family kept it that way. And the flowers on his grave were always replaced before they withered. But that day they visited, Maria brought a flowering plant with a pot from Lili's garden. She said they all now have a reason to visit him every day because the plant needed to be watered daily.

"What plant did you uproot from my garden?" Lili complained.

Maria declared it was a pink rain lily.

"Rain lilies do not die easily. It can survive even the longest drought."

Edward asked, "So why rain lily?"

"Because our friendship survived the longest drought. It did not die easily."

Lili Crossman cried in silence while the two stated their prayers in secret.

Chapter Twenty-Five

Katarin Kristova was home again. She was running and calling Antonia who occupied herself doing whatever in the vineyard. "Antonia! I came with Aunt Maria! Come quickly now!"

"I'm coming! I'm coming!" replied the twin sister whose hair now was longer and more vibrant under the sun. "What is the rush?"

Madam Maria met Antonia at the entrance of the vineyard. The former was too excited for what's going to happen that day. Katarin left the two to have their private conversation.

"Aunt Maria, welcome!" greeted Antonia.

"Why did you never write to me?" asked the madam who was panting from the long walk. "I used to be your human diary."

"The vineyard took all of my time."

"You are not a good liar, Antonia. Pour the tea."

"Well," Antonia began. "I was guilty about what happened. I caused trouble. And because of me, Elric almost died."

"But Elric is alive, Antonia. You have the chance to fight for your love. I am the one who should have been kinder and forgiving and understanding, but I wasn't."

"Yet I was stubborn."

"Fine. But don't blame yourself. Let us share the burden to lighten up your load. And please know that I love you very much. So, make time to send me letters, alright?"

"I promise."

"Now, now. I must inform you about important guests visiting you today." Madam Kristova shifted her way to a carriage a half-mile distant.

"What did you do this time, grandma?"

"You will see."

Edward Coldwell did all the talking while sitting beside his nephew who was looking sullen inside the carriage they were boarding.

"Forgive me, Elric. I only did what I thought was the right thing," made the nephew realize he was with someone and was going somewhere he did not even have the strength to ask about.

"No worries, uncle. I just want to punish myself for being indecisive. I should have avoided her at all. It was I who insisted on the friendship. Look where it led us, almost death. I'm glad I'm only colorblind without killing her in the process."

"Stop the punishment, Elric. I have been doing that, too, upon myself. For many years actually. And it ruined my soul."

"But I think Antonia won't accept me. I don't feel complete anymore. And maybe she won't forgive me for everything that's happened."

"How sure are you that she's blaming you about everything and not herself for making you blind?"

"I don't know. I just think I lost my chance. Or maybe she did not like me to begin with. She actually never said good bye when she left."

"Are you certain you lost the chance? You were the one who did not accept her visitation when you were under observation. She wanted to see you but you refused. She wrote letters you did not even try to reply. What if she's also feeling guilty just like you? What will you do?" were the questions which left Elric thinking as the carriage halted. "And how sure are you that she did not feel the same thing towards you when in fact you did not even tell her your feelings directly? And you ask for a good bye? A good bye? Really now, Elric? Are you even sure you want to say good bye to her?"

Elric remained speechless even until he went out of the carriage. He saw a familiar house right after and thought he saw Antonia but realized eventually it was her twin sister, Katarin. "Hello, Miss Katarin!" he greeted.

"You can see," Katarin gasped. "That is good to hear."

"Do you live here?"

"Yes, this is our home."

"Captain Kallistar is your father? Oh, good lord!"

"Father likes you, do not fear," Katarin smiled. "So how did you know it was I and not my twin?"

"Though I am colorblind, I can still see red. And your hair isn't."

"That is odd but I adore it. Come, Mr Coldwell! I'll take you to Antonia."

Rudolf Kristov appeared and welcomed Edward Coldwell with a tight hug. "Welcome to my home, Sir Coldwell."

"I cannot believe to be here again in Ardia. Thank you for letting us be here."

"I believe 'tis time to meddle with the children's cold war."

At the entrance of the vineyard, Antonia was standing beside Madam Kristova. Both women were surprised when they saw Elric and Katarin walking towards them.

"Madam Kristova, good day! It appears to me you have planned this together with Uncle Edward. I should have known." Elric was talking about how his uncle dragged him to the countryside for a retreat.

"I know nothing, young lad," Madam Kristova lied. "And since you are here, Katarin and I must take our exit." Both paraded out of the scene when Katarin concurred with her grandmother.

Antonia began pacing along the grapevines, Elric followed. She did not know what to say and was guilty of even talking with him. She tried to forget his face for the past few months, only for him to reappear all of a sudden.

Elric noticed she was walking barefoot but still looked like a nymph surrounded by nature. "Your hair looks more vibrant than before," he said, whispering.

"And you did not become blind."

"I have colorblindness, nonetheless."

"But how did you know my hair is red again? Aren't you supposed to see only black and white and grey?"

"Yes, but I can also see red. I don't know why. I used to hate red when I was a child but I adore it now. It's as if a miracle happened."

"That's good to hear, isn't it?"

"Yes, yes," Elric was nervous. "How are you?"

"Hmm, I had no time to do other things than work at my winery. I must busy myself in order for my mind to never entertain thoughts and imaginings which would lead me hoping again for things and people I cannot attain."

Silence befell them. Antonia was hopeless while Elric was brimming with hope. "Can we be friends again, Antonia?" His heart was trembling.

"I cannot," Antonia answered without any second thoughts. "I cannot do it anymore, Elric. Being friends with you is terrible."

Elric's spirit fell to the ground. He expected such an answer but still hoped for a positive one. Now he was all red and he wanted to run. Away from her, and as far as he could.

"Can you at least tell me why?" He needed an explanation. "Are you blaming me that you almost died?"

"That is not what I meant, Elric!" she turned to him. "You misunderstood my words. I cannot blame you for what's happened because I have been feeling guilty since then. If I did not tell you about Expedition VII, you would have been fine. And not what you are now, colorblind."

"But I am fine," he insisted. "I have my sight even though I am colorblind. Tell me, why did you never say good bye? Am I not worthy of a proper farewell even as a friend or an acquaintance? Is it because I became blind? Is it because I am not the Elric you used to know anymore?"

"No, no, no, no, no!" she said aloud, almost singing. In a second, she palmed his crimsoned cheek. "You're over-analyzing things, Elric. I never said my farewells because I never wanted to. Besides, you never wanted to see me, too. And good bye meant not seeing you again. I despise never seeing you again. I was guilty, I was afraid you'd blame me for everything that had happened. That's why I stopped writing to you after receiving no replies. I felt too guilty for you being blind."

Elric held her hand and held it warmly as if he was holding a precious stone he could never let go. "It's not your fault, Antonia. I am actually glad I only lost my sight at the time and not you. But I think I did lose you."

"Lose me? What are you trying to say?" she giggled.

"It's nothing."

"I don't think it is nothing."

"Then tell me first why we cannot be friends anymore."

She gently told him. "Of course, you know. Of all people, Elric, you know. Must I be the one to tell? Have you forgotten about it already?"

"I know nothing. Just tell me, please. I want my pain to end. This meeting is hurting me so much that I want to just vanish from your sight."

"Oh, Elric," she hesitated to validate if her father's claim of Elric's affection for her was true. So, she just stated it. "My father believed you are in love with me. You spoke, yes? While you were here helping him restore our home."

"Oh," Elric wasn't able to act innocent. "That."

"Was he mistaken?"

Elric rejoiced. Now he understood why they could never be friends. "This is really embarrassing."

"Perhaps, it is true," Antonia smiled.

"You are too blunt about it, because you don't feel the same. That's why you're making fun of me."

"That is completely an absurd way of asking the woman you love if she has the same feelings for you, is it not?"

"Then will you marry me?"

"Are you not too hasty about that now? You're not even sure they'll support us. Besides, your uncle and my great-aunt love each other dearly."

"I bet they will let us marry. It was my uncle who dragged me here. I didn't even know where our destination was to begin with. Then what a small world it is. Captain Kallistar is your father."

Antonia smirked. "So how's my place?"

"Compelling."

"One more thing, though. That time in your room, you wanted to kiss me, did you not?"

"Oh! That was the one which made a scandal around the capital that I was into men."

"I shared the same rumor, of course. I was into women because you used Elisa's name just to send me letters."

"I did want to kiss you at that time. I was just afraid you'd kill me if I did without your consent."

"You can ask me now."

"May I?"

"May what?"

"You're doing it again."

"Do what?"

"Teasing me."

"You have to live with it."

"I am glad to, Antonia," Elric hid a smile before hugging his dear Antonia. "I surely am."

Antonia pulled Elric's hand, the one with a faded scar on the palm, and kissed it. "Well I am more glad to have met you that night. It was laughable yet unforgettable."

"Was it love at first fight?"

"Did you not know? I put a spell on you." Antonia grinned as she circled Elric's ring finger with her curly red locks.

"I am most glad you did so," he smiled almost trying to touch his face with hers.

Antonia then pulled Elric's collar, whispering, "Come here, you. Your lips are cold," and kissed him.

The two remained engaged to be married for three years before deciding to be wrapped by the band of unity in front of the people important to them. Elric continued his liquor trading business while pursuing his painting career from time to time even though he was colorblind. He used the pseudonym Flavus and his works became famous all over the country. The red color was his main thing and Antonia was his muse every time.

Antonia began writing novels, too, while managing her winery. All of her stories were about people who did not conform to the norms of society, like her. Most of her main characters were women with odd interests and dreams. Though some of her works were publicized, a few did not see the light. Yet she had kept them, for she believed that one day those works would make their way out of the dark. Her pen name was Antoine Noir.

-- THE END --

About the Author

Judel B. Nuique

Judel B. Nuique is a Cebuano-speaking Negrense who was born and raised in Santa Catalina, a town in the southern part of the Negros Island. She is the only daughter to sugarcane farmers in a family of four. She graduated a Magna Cum Laude in 2015, and passed both civil service examination and licensure examination for professional teachers that same year. She worked as an online ESL teacher in Metro Manila to Korean and Japanese clients abroad before the pandemic. Yet after the pandemic she decided to settle in her hometown to pursue her teaching profession. Though she always considered herself a poet and an artist, the pandemic turned her into a novelist. She is an August Virgo, a shape shifter, and an NBSB for three decades.

www.ingramcontent.com/pod-product-compliance
Lightning Source LLC
LaVergne TN
LVHW041924070526
838199LV00051BA/2721